FOUR JEWISH BRIDES

Liora Ayalon

Producer & International Distributor
eBookPro Publishing
www.ebook-pro.com

FOUR JEWISH BRIDES
Liora Ayalon
Copyright © 2023 Liora Ayalon

All rights reserved; No parts of this book may be
reproduced or transmitted in any form or by any means,
electronic or mechanical, including photocopying,
recording, taping, or by any information retrieval system,
without the permission, in writing, of the author.

Translation: Judith Yacov
Editing: Elisheva Lahav

Contact: liora5577@gmail.com

ISBN 9798872826491

Four Jewish Brides

A Novel

LIORA AYALON

In revealing the story of Jacob Isaac, the "Holy Jew,"
I searched for the soul, spirit, and melody
of his grandson – my father, Jacob.
In memory of my beloved father,
Jacob Finkelstein O.B.M.
1924 – 1968

Contents

INSTEAD OF AN INTRODUCTION

There was a man, and he had a wife.

And I said to myself: Look for the wife.

Each time one of my sons read his bar mitzvah portion, he recalled our family roots and proudly announced:

"We are the descendants of Jacob Isaac, the Holy Jew of Peshischa." We knew that he was a righteous man, the Holy Jew of Peshischa, and we also knew that he had established the Peshischa Hassidic Court, but beyond that, we knew nothing.

We were told that a street in Jaffa was once named for the Holy Jew. Arabs occupied the neighborhood. At first, we found that amusing, but later we were angry that, of all places, it had been decided to name the street after "The Jew" in an Arab neighborhood, because we felt that it was perhaps intended to annoy the residents. However, the committee that selects the street names in the city of Tel Aviv-Jaffa decided to change the name of the street at one of its meetings, and since then it isn't named after our Jacob Isaac.

And we were familiar with the history of the Hassidic courts. When we studied Hebrew literature at university, we read *In Praise of the Baal Shem Tov* and explored the generations of his heirs and their teachings; among them was *The Seer of Lublin*, whom we knew had been one of

9

the Jew's teachers, and about Menachem Mendel of Kotzk, who was a disciple of The Jew. But we didn't hear a word about The Jew himself. Therefore we continued searching and examining, and were delighted to discover that Martin Buber wrote his novel, *Gog and Magog* (Armageddon), about the complicated relationship between two righteous men, Hassidic leaders with the same name: Jacob Isaac, i.e., Jacob Isaac Horowitz, The Seer of Lublin, and his disciple, Jacob Isaac Rabinowitz, our "Jew" – the Holy Jew of Peshischa. As soon as this was revealed to us in the research literature, we eagerly read the book.

When *Gog and Magog* was published in a new edition, edited by Dov Elbaum, we rushed to buy copies for all the family members. Once again I was captivated by the novel and read it fervently. And here, in this second reading, I was amazed when the author bothered to mention the wife of The Jew only when he needed her as a scapegoat. For example, when something or someone was not appropriately dressed, it was immediately explained that she – the wife – was responsible for that: "The garment itself lacks something. It is something that, if it exists, the garment is wearable. And if it is missing, the garment is not wearable" (in the words of Agnon in his story "The Garment.").[1] She always spoils everything – such as in everyday affairs and matters of the soul; she even intervenes in the upper worlds, and even for the worse. She spoils everything. And who will ruin even the coming of the Messiah? The wife of "The Holy Jew of Peshischa."

---

1. In Shmuel Yosef Agnon's symbolic scheme, the garment represents the soul.

And I said to myself: *Cherchez la femme!* Big-time.

I thought about her, the young one who married her dead sister's husband, and she was said to have blamed her brother-in-law – who became her husband – for her sister's death. I pondered her impossible situation of living in the shadow of the righteous man – the widower of the sister you loved – the life of a woman married to a man who leads his life and, within it also the life of his family, according to clear yet harsh principles that at times are somewhat blind and domineering. The extent to which The Jew of Peshischa was a man of principles sometimes made him seem so righteous that he appeared to lose other human attributes, like mercy and compassion. And my father taught me that according to Hillel the Elder, the central tenet of Judaism is "Love thy neighbor as thyself." Perhaps, precisely because of this, because he was a man of intellect, of sharp, incisive, and piercing principles, our "Jew" was ignored by most of the books that researched the generations of the righteous leaders who came after the Baal Shem Tov, and that despite being the founder of the Hassidic Court of Peshischa, a magnificent Hassidic movement from which many such Hassidic courts arose, e.g., the Kotzk, Gur, Porisov, and the Biala Hassids – despite the admiration of his disciples and being a close friend of the compassionate, merciful Rabbi David of Lelov. Perhaps because of that, because of his excessive erudition, the well-known scholars skip over him in their books, and after Rabbi Elimelech of Lizhensk, they write about The Seer of Lublin, the teacher of The Jew and then about some other righteous leader, each according to his taste, and continue to Rabbi Simcha Bunim, The Jew's disciple, and on the way they lost sight of our Jew. At any

11

rate, it cannot be that they didn't know him or know that he was the rabbi and teacher of Rabbi Simcha Bunim, who continued the lineage of the Peshischa Hassidic tradition with its abstract method of study. Yet when they do write about him, about our Jew, they show a clear preference for The Seer, who is described as one who understood that his role as a righteous leader was to show benevolence – that is, to mediate between the earthly and the Divine abundance and work miracles for the benefit of his followers, as opposed to our Jew, who is described as someone who believes in personal responsibility and therefore avoids performing miracles, and avoids doing so in principle, even when such a miracle may redeem and rescue. He avoids such actions to the extent that he refuses to use his power as a righteous man to help the masses of weak and oppressed who come to his door. Out of decency and a deep sense of equality, he even refuses to revive the sick son of The Seer of Lublin, supposedly because the boy's mother used to defame him when speaking to The Seer and disobeyed The Jew when he ordered her to stop inciting and turning The Seer against him. And here, once more, is a revelation of a woman spoiling things, and again The Jew turns out to be cold and devoid of compassion.

Then I thought that perhaps our Jew disappeared from the scholars' view because he did not put his words and new ideas into writing and even instructed his followers not to write down his words. The reason, he claimed, was that writing about his innovations in books taints them when it piles commentary upon commentary. Therefore he did not put his words and innovative ideas into writing, since doing so would kill their vitality and conceal their soul.

It was essential for The Jew to call attention to the need to renew himself at every moment and avoid fixation on any specific moment. To this end, he was called "The Jew" because he wanted to convert each day anew from someone who had not yet achieved the primary goal of becoming a complete Jew.

I also noticed that the scholars who nevertheless delved into the character of The Jew, surprisingly tended to be fond of him. So, for example, Dov Elbaum, who edited "*Gog and Magog*" in its new edition, followed Martin Buber in this matter and identified with The Jew, according to the literary critics who wrote about the book – and to my feeling, too. "The man of the market," he called him, a simple man who would give the shirt off his back to a poor man, even if that shirt had been a gift from his teacher and spiritual leader, The Seer. A man who doesn't leave a penny to lie overnight in his house but gives everything he has and all that is left over – if indeed anything is left over, to the poor – a man who is modest and humble enough to go out to beg for alms in the market and talk to the women there while he did so. There is much genuine compassion in these actions; it was tangible physical compassion, and not just by way of a miracle. Following this, I thought of valid and false images and the interpretation that could slant in one direction. Still, I knew another thing: Even if The Jew was a man of compassion, as I believed him to be, he did not necessarily treat the members of his household compassionately.

Because I thought once more about his wife, Sheindel, and how difficult it was to always live in poverty and agree to follow her husband's dictate not to leave a spare penny in her home and give everything one has to others, even not knowing if your children would have anything to eat to-morrow, I decided to examine her character. The historical truth revealed in Hassidic stories and even in researchers' conclusions is unfair to Sheindel. I remember the distinction that Ahad Ha'am made between historical and archeological truth. Historical truth is the truth as you recall it, how it influences the course of your life and shapes your worldview. In contrast, archeological truth is the one that is discovered when studying the facts themselves, inasmuch as they become clear to us, and I sought Sheindel's truth, leaving me no choice but to seek the archeological truth.

After all, the things told in the tales and studies all match the attitude of Judaism toward women in that peri-od – and in the view of that Hassidic Judaism – that the woman is the source of evil. Trouble came into the world only because of a woman. All evil began with the image of Eve when a snake tempted her. And some claim that she se-duced the snake because, like all women, she was a tempt-ress. I have a hard time understanding that judgment. Isn't the wife supposed to be her husband's helpmate? Or is the woman's role summed up as a background of evil and cor-ruption that sharpens the righteousness of the righteous leader? All I want is to be able to understand Sheindel and how she understood the events. But how can I differentiate between truth and fiction? How can I distinguish between a reality that suits my worldview and one that does not? With the rush of so many thoughts, I could not put things in writing.

Until the dreams came and the effort to find objective truth became strange and unnecessary, I began to tell things as they were revealed in my visions.

FOUR JEWISH BRIDES

I often dreamt the same dream. The same four Jewish brides repeatedly appear in that dream.

The four of them are dressed in white. Four beautiful young brides. Four smiling, laughing brides. A soft light illuminates them.

Two of them stand, the third is seated, and the fourth leans over her. They are preoccupied with themselves and unaware of what is happening around them.

And I, who has dreamt and watched them, am also not seen by them. I draw closer to the four of them and ask to belong, to join in their joy, and notice that the material from which their clothes are woven resembles a net. I take a few more steps toward them and see that their white clothes are no more than shrouds. White shrouds, some of which have crumbled. The smell of death suddenly permeates my consciousness, and I understand that all four are no longer alive. How did the stench of death become recognizable to me? I have never experienced death because in our day, as it is known, only very few people come face to face with death and are familiar with its odor. Medical students, for example, or morticians. In the past, the image and odor of death were more accessible when epidemics like smallpox and the Bubonic Plague wrought havoc and destruction on the world, with carts loaded with corpses and harnessed to men. And while I still dream of the four women, the memory that comes to mind is of the stench of death I read about in *The Brothers Karamazov*, when the ascetic – Zossima, the retired monk – passed away.

Except in my dream, the odor is faint and not at all repulsive. It doesn't even raise any doubts regarding the priest's righteousness and adherence to the strictest rules.

The four brides form a circle and start dancing. Although the atmosphere around them is joyful, I can't help but recall the song they used to sing during the Bubonic Plague, and I almost expect to hear it burst out of their mouths:

> *Ring-a-round the Rosie*
> *A pocket full of posies*
> *Ashes! Ashes! We all fall down.*

But, no. Their voices are not heard, and they only go around in the circle. From close by, I notice that their dancing is not dancing, but more like floating because those who are no longer alive can hover above the ground. I have an inner awareness of being bonded to these four women, with ties of love, and I want to meld with them and turn myself into a presence in the reality that they exist. Because I do not doubt it, I know them, but I cannot recognize even one of them. Perhaps I knew them once when they were already old women, wrinkled, and in pain?

How have they become so happy?

And how are they so young?

When I approach the circle, I am no longer a woman, but a girl in a white dress with a rabbit and a carrot embroidered on the bodice. I can tell they are happy to welcome me, and when they understand that I don't recognize them, they introduce themselves to me, one after the other. One says, "I'm Sheindel," and I stare at her. Her nose is long, her face is not beautiful, and she carries herself as if she knows what lies ahead and is ready to struggle with difficulty. Then Sheindel points to the woman standing next to her, and I look at her and see how beautiful she is. Sheindel doesn't introduce her by name but says,

"This is my big sister."

Then she points to the third woman, whose hair is pitch black and whose eyes dart around all the time, looking for something important, and says,

"This is Beilah."

Finally, she points to the fourth – a skinny, bony woman with fair hair and a vertical scar on her forehead – and says,

"We don't know the name of this one. We thought of calling her 'Warp,' as in the cross threads 'warp and woof' because of the scar on her forehead, but perhaps we had better call her Miriam..."

They join hands again and go around in a circle. They invite me to dance with them but I refuse. No, I'm not ready to join them yet. Not yet.

Sheindel smiles despite my refusal, then turns to me and says, "We know why you came to us. We'll tell you the story you're asking to hear, and you'll pass it on to others in your own words. There is no need to exert yourself and write a period novel in the formal language of the past. Write the story in your own words, as if you were relating it to yourself or someone close to you. Are you wondering where we pick up notions like 'a period novel?' Child, here we know everything. We also know what we don't know. And out of our story will arise the images of two who separated us in our lifetime and reunited us in our death. Each of them bears the name 'Jacob Isaac.' One is Jacob Isaac, who, in our time, was known as 'The Jew,' and in your time was described as 'The Holy Jew.' He was her husband – she points to the sister who is more beautiful than she – and afterwards was *my* husband, and was also Beilah's nightmare. The other is Jacob Isaac, known as 'The Seer of Lublin.' He was the husband of Beilah and the nightmare of Warp. 'The Jew,' our Jacob Isaac, was handsome and clever, a great leader and man of principles. Having principles is a beautiful thing, but try and imagine what it's like to be the wife of such a man, one who lives only and exclusively for his ideals, a man for whom his principles are more important than his well-being or that of the members of his family. . . a man who demands more and more of himself all the time to keep to the ideals he chose, who dedicates his life and that of those who live alongside him to achieving the unattainable goal that he identifies as 'the work of the Almighty.' And no more but that he believes with all his heart that all he has achieved until now in his work has no value and is worth no more than the peel of a clove of garlic. Every day he must begin anew, like Sisyphus climbing the mountain. And 'The Seer,' their Jacob Isaac, was confident that he would be able to see and understand everything, although in fact, there was no one blinder than he. Their story is woven into the story of our lives. But this time, our story – the women's story – will be central, and all the events that took place will be presented from our point of view. And believe me, as opposed to the Jacob Isaacs, our vision is more acute."

That is what Sheindel told me in my dream.

And after I dreamt the dream once and once again, I decided to examine and find out who those women were. Sheindel did not call her sister by name but introduced her as her older sister. I checked the written sources and read about Jacob Isaac of Peshischa, the "Holy Jew." From the many stories and articles written about him, I also learned about "The Seer of Lublin" and the relationship between the two of them. They were both considered righteous spiritual leaders; in the writings about them, reference is also made to their wives. But it was not without reason that Sheindel did not mention her sister's name, the name of the first wife of The Jew – a great, righteous man and leader of his followers – whose own name is not mentioned anywhere. That is the fate of the wife, I thought. Even when married to a virtuous man, her name will likely be forgotten.

But only sometimes, of course, since the wives of most of the righteous leaders of the period were mentioned by name. For example, the second wife of The Seer was Tehila Shprintze, daughter of Rabbi Tzvi Hirsh, except that The Seer did not particularly like Tehila Shprintze and kept her hidden away. When he looked into the face of her predecessor – his first wife – he noticed the warp and the woof marks on her forehead and found that they resembled a crucifix; as a result, he left her immediately after their marriage. Her name is also unknown, so, as the four dancing women did, we will call her Miriam. Of Tehila Shprintze it is said that The Seer could not bring himself to look at her.

That wasn't because there was something terrible or off-putting about her soul, but because her body and face were not pleasing enough in his view. After all, he was a great man of virtue who could look into the soul, the source of any person's soul, and know whether they were of the seed of Cain or of Abel. Here, despite his eminence, he wholeheartedly believed that women were intended to broaden the mindset of the righteous leader. Their physical beauty was no less – and perhaps more – important than the beauty of their souls; therefore he was put off by his wife, and when she died he rushed to marry the beautiful Beilah. It is told that each time Beilah's brother came to The Seer and asked him whether a particular marriage offer was or was not suitable for her, The Seer said it was not and determined that she deserved a better match, according to what he could see in the heavens. Because whom did he see in the sky? He saw himself. And when Tehila Shprintze went to her eternal rest, he hurried to fulfill what he had seen in the heavens and took Beilah to be his wife.

So here it turns out there are wives of the righteous leaders who are mentioned by their names, like Tehila Shprintze and Beilah. This was also the fate of Rivka, the wife of Simcha Bunim, The Tzadik,[2] who inherited the leadership of the Peshischa Hassids after The Jew departed this life. Whether she was beautiful or ugly was never discussed there. What was important was that she was wise and was a friend in heart and soul to her husband, Simcha Bunim. He sought her advice in all matters, and they were so close that their love resembled the love between the Baal Shem Tov and his wife, Hannah, the sister of Rabbi Abraham Gershon of Kitov. Hannah was also a second wife. From

---

2. A leader of Hassidism is called *tzadik, or* "righteous" due to his personal prestige and moral position and because of his charismatic relationship with the Divine world.

his first wife, the Baal Shem Tov had no children. It is also told that before the Baal Shem Tov married Hannah, he revealed his secret to her, that he was a hidden righteous man whose status would be revealed in the future. He did not want his relationship with his wife to be blemished by a secret. He wanted their love to be exposed and open.

And here are the names of two first wives – the first wife of the first Jacob Isaac and the second Jacob Isaac – that were forgotten. And if it was said of Warp, the first wife of The Seer, which is Miriam, who bore no children, that a terrible secret shrouded her life, perhaps we can rationalize why her name was forgotten. After all, the first wife of the Holy Jew of Peshischa actually had children, and there wasn't even a secret that clouded her life. So how do we explain the fact that her name was also lost?

In Buber's *Gog and Magog*, Sheindel's older sister is called Feigaleh, Tzipporah, perhaps because of her weakness and delicate birdlike nature. In the family trees and historical records that I researched, I found that her name was Breindel. But after going a bit deeper, I discovered that Breindel was her granddaughter.

I also learned that not only did the names of the wives sometimes disappear from the stories of the righteous leaders, but so did the names of the daughters, and when one tries to understand who the children of the righteous leaders were, it becomes clear that only the sons' names are recorded. I wondered how The Holy Jew had only three sons from two wives – Yerachmiel from the first wife, and Yehoshua-Asher and Nechemiah from the second. Was there only one child from his first wife? After all, it is noted that when The Jew went on his travels while he was still married to his first wife, she had difficulty providing for the children on her own. "Children" was written in the plural, and I understood that there were also daughters whom they didn't count or mention by name. I researched and found that one was called Rivka Rachel, and I didn't find the name of the other one. The only thing that is told about her is that she was married to Raphaels Shmuel of Yosepov; it is also said that her daughter – the granddaughter of The Jew – was married to Abraham Moshe Bonhardt, the Holy Prodigy, the son of Simcha Bunim. The name of this daughter was Breindel, the same Breindel who was raised in the home of her grandmother and grandfather – who, were, of course, The Jew and Sheindel. Finally, was the name of the daughter of The Jew not mentioned because she died in the prime of her life? It may be safe to presume that the daughter named her own daughter for her late mother; thus, from here on we'll call the first wife of the Holy Jew by two names: Breindel-Feigaleh.

TWO SISTERS

Four Jewish Brides.

The four of them are dressed in white. Four beautiful young brides. Four smiling, laughing brides. A soft light illuminates them.

Two of them stand, the third is seated, and the fourth leans over her. They are preoccupied with themselves and unaware of what is happening around them. Their white clothes are no more than shrouds. White shrouds, some of them have crumbled. The four form a circle and start dancing; their movements resemble floating. The two sisters, Sheindel and Breindel-Feigaleh, enter the circle, and Sheindel says, "Listen, and I will tell you the story of our childhood."

And so Sheindel told us.

Each time a son was born, Father would name him. He would choose from the names of relatives, sages, rabbis he respected, esteemed authors, or Biblical heroes.

But when it was a daughter, the mother was the one who named her. When my older sister was born, my mother had difficulty with her birth. For many hours, the infant struggled to enter the world, and when at long last she was born, Mother looked at her and saw a black-haired baby, her face red from the effort of the difficult birth, and tiny like a chick.

23

So Mother named her Breindel Feigaleh. Breindel, because of her black hair and red face, and Feigaleh, Tzipporah,[3] because she was so small and fragile. And indeed, when the day came to name her, our mother noticed how quiet she was and how little she cried, as well as the pale color of her eyes, and knew that the name Breindel-Feigaleh suited her more than any other possibly could since Breindel means "tawny," and is also close to the name Bruria, which means "clear" or "distinct." And she was also dark-haired, tiny like a bird, and spread a calmness to everyone around her. It was easy to see that she would not use her elbows to fight for her place in the world.

When I was born, I was bigger than the other babies she bore; my hair was lighter, my eyes were blue, and my cheeks were rosy. Joy entered my father's heart when he saw me and said, "Nu, a sheine maideleh, she's a beautiful baby." And so when Mother saw Father's joy, she named me Sheindel Freideh. Sheindel because of the beauty, and Freideh because of Father's joy and the pleasure I gave. Apparently my mother believed that I was a beautiful baby, and worthy of the name Sheindel, because she found a resemblance to her face in mine. Some mothers search for themselves in their children and love themselves in them. Don't make a face. Some women do that, and my mother found herself in my face. My character also bore similarities to hers – the same determination, obstinate fighting spirit, and the fact that I never gave up on what I desired. And my mother didn't know that she also directed the paths of our lives with the

---

3, In Hebrew and in Yiddish, the name Feigaleh is derived from a word meaning bird.

names she gave us and didn't foresee the great confusion and strange changes of fate that our names heralded for us.

And indeed, Feigaleh was fragile like a bird; when her life hit rough times, she was like a bird with broken wings. In contrast, what happened to me is what usually happens to babies named Sheineh, meaning beauty. I grew up to be a girl who looked pretty usual rather than unusually pretty, and some would say, "She lacks a little charm." How cruel – or at least ironic that name was for me – mainly because my sister Feigaleh was so beautiful. I admired her, especially as she grew up and began to wear her hair in one long braid instead of two, as was the custom for girls. I would look at her and express pride in her beauty to my girlfriends, especially on Sabbath evenings when she strolled with her companions.

Yet I, with my big nose, was named Sheineh. And Mother loved me so much. When she was preparing the marital bed on the wedding day of her firstborn daughter, Feigaleh, she saw me through the window, with my hair blowing wild as I ran, trying to join in a game of hide-and-seek with my brothers. They, however, refused to include me in their games and sent me to play with the rag doll my mother had made for me.

She immediately felt sorry for me and called me to help her with her work, and prayed from the depths of her heart, "If only my daughter Sheindel is lucky enough to get a husband like Jacob Isaac, this good-hearted, clever, gentle hero." Did she realize what she was praying for? Had she prepared a bridal bed for Feigaleh or a death bed? Because of this prayer, as Jacob Isaac later said, a blessing that flowed from a pure heart, Feigaleh was doomed to a better world to make room for me and fulfill my mother's wish for her daughter Sheindel to find a husband like him. This story never convinced me, since my mother used the word "like," meaning she never intended for me to marry Jacob Isaac himself, but rather someone like him. Thus, I did not rush to blame my mother for my beloved sister's death. I blamed him – her husband, Jacob Isaac – for her death, but I'm getting ahead of myself.

In that long-ago era, our childhood days were wonderful and pleasant. We had plenty and were short of nothing; my father worked in the tavern. However, there was no resemblance between our inn and the one described in Bialik's[4] poem "My Father" as a "den of piggish men" (and don't ask how I know about Bialik – as I have already explained – where we exist it is possible to read and understand everything, and there is no "before" and no "after.") Father stood behind the counter like a landlord and did not wear the "skull of a holy martyr." However, we, the members of his household, knew full well that even though his fellowmen behaved honorably towards him and he made a good living, he lived in constant fear of the alcohol-fueled pogroms,[5] because each such event was prone to wreak greater havoc and lead to more significant damage and expensive repairs. All that added to the increasing real, deep apprehension of a possible attack on us – the sons and daughters of the family.

---

4. Hayim Nahman Bialik is recognized as the national poet of the State of Israel.

5. Pogrom is a Russian word meaning "to wreak havoc, to demolish violently." Historically, the term refers to violent attacks by local non-Jewish populations on Jews in the Russian Empire and other European countries.

During my childhood, the noise of the tavern would enter my dreams and permeate my consciousness. Whenever a drunk lost his temper and a rampage broke out, we children were immediately ordered to hide in the storeroom attic. Our house was too far from those of the village people, who preferred to live close to one another, and it stood alone; an expansive courtyard led to the adjacent parking area for wagons. In the early days of winter, the parking area was covered with sticky mud, but as the cold intensified, it would be covered with snow that remained white for the first few days until stained from wagon wheels and visitors' footprints. In the parking area lived a blacksmith named Andrzej, who shoed the horses parked there, and I loved watching him work. Andrzej would grasp the hoof and nails with one hand and the horse's leg with the other; as he worked, he spoke to the horse with a great tenderness that was in complete contrast to the aggression that radiated from the powerful image that he projected. He was extremely tall, and his body was broad.

"You are a fine horse," he would say, "and I only want to help you. We are close relatives, from the same family…" He also repaired the wagon wheels and various tools the villagers brought him. He was industrious, and we would wake up to the pounding of his hammer in the morning.

The tavern itself stood behind the parking area – a dark building with a wide entrance and narrow windows, and behind it was our house, with its narrow door and wide windows; between the residence and field behind it stood the barn, which contained fodder for the horses, and in which we also put the apples and tubers (which they also called potatoes), because there wasn't enough storage space in the kitchen. At that point, a gap between the barn's ceiling and the roof wasn't visible to someone standing in the barn, and one could hide in it. We would climb up to the opening using a heavy wooden ladder. Each time we used it, we lifted it with our combined strength and stored it in the hiding place so that nothing of the climb would be known. No one would be able to figure out where we were hiding. Father had a particular sign. Whenever he was startled by some drunken guest, he would start rubbing his left ear hard, and we would understand the hint and rush off to hide in the barn's attic.

Toward Passover, when we girls helped Mother with the preparations for the holiday, there were hints from Father that grew more frequent. Each time they got together, a group of men would come to the tavern on some secret mission, whisper to one another, and sniff at the wine without tasting it. Father would grow apprehensive of a blood libel, especially if, in the preceding days, a dead day-old infant had been found on the banks of the river. There were more than a few incidents of gentile girls who had given birth premaritally and drowned their babies in the river.

The river would freeze in winter, and the layer of ice covered the lives cut short. Towards spring, the snow would melt, and suddenly the body of an infant would be seen floating in the water. The time of death was unknown because the freezing cold water prevented the little bodies from decomposing.

When the unfortunate infant was found during the days close to the Passover, the gentiles and Jews, too, would recall the dastardly stories of blood libel that took place in the distant past, either many years before or more recently.

When the men came to the tavern close to the Passover festival, they were already well-primed with alcohol. They poked their noses suspiciously into what they were being served and were in no hurry to imbibe it. Father would be anxious and send the brothers to gather his children. With bated breath, we would climb up to the barn's roof.

It was spring, the season when my grandmother would tell us about the good and bad events that befell her and others in her youth, and they included stories of the libels like the one that occurred in our city, Apt. And just when my father noted that the inebriated men were whispering among themselves, and his suspicion was aroused, the two of us – Feigaleh and I – entered the tavern. A mischievous spirit took hold of us that day. The birch trees had put forth white buds, and the sky was bright blue with a few wispy clouds floating above. On the ground, the beautiful grass was green. We wore summery dresses without heavy winter coats. We felt light and free, and began to chase each other. My sister's hair was in two braids that surrounded her head like a circle; my two braids always unravel, and Mother tries to keep them in place with hairpins. My sister is taller than I am; her limbs are already curvy, while I have a slim frame and am almost skinny. My slimness gives me an advantage because I am faster than she is, and whenever we have a race, I reach the goal first. We both laugh about nothing, and I brag and promise her that I will always get there first, while she, my big sister, will be so far behind that not a trace of her will be left!

And, with the same springtime enthusiasm, we burst into the tavern together; inside it was an unpleasant cold-ness. The steam clouding the room came from the samovar, from which strong, hot tea was poured for the guests. The windows were closed, and only a little bit of light penetrated the room. Straggly hairy men with whiskered faces sat or huddled there, frowning at us with wrinkled brows without a glimmer of a smile, measuring us from head to foot, their gazes pausing especially on my older sister, on the blush of her cheeks, her sparkling white teeth that were revealed between her pink lips, and lower down to her hips.

Father, who caught on to their glances immediately, caught a fright and hurriedly signaled to us to get out and disappear — except that in his fear, he forgot the familiar code, and instead of energetically rubbing his ear, he just said, "Go to Mother right away and help her prepare a hot meal for the visitors," and I failed to grasp his intention. Nevertheless, I hurried after Feigaleh, who rushed out of the tavern, ran to the barn, and was already climbing the ladder when she whispered to me, 'Let's see who gets left behind now. Be quiet. Be quick. Be careful. Let's hope those "Tartars" don't catch you and finish you off.'"

Only Grandmother used the word Tartars, so the word was enough to remind me of all her terrifying stories of blood libel. I knew that they were gentiles who persecuted the Jews and made up stories about them, especially on days like this, in the springtime. I couldn't breathe and couldn't move.

"Quickly!" my sister urged me. "Don't hurt your leg again! And don't let your legs get caught in your dress! Be careful and hurry!"

And immediately after I managed to climb the ladder, shaking all over, she continued to make me run:

"Stop daydreaming, Sheindel! You have to climb the

30

ladder and make room for it… Here, lie on the beam and be careful not to fall … Yes, like that. Fast… It's bad enough that you are so small and can't help pick up the heavy ladder, so if you're so small, at least don't take up too much space…"

Again, I couldn't breathe, and fear choked me up. In my dream, I am larger, stronger, and nimbler, and I quickly dash to the barn. The darkness doesn't frighten me because my eyes have grown accustomed to it. The sunlight doesn't blind me, so I don't blink like someone half blind when I go into the dark barn, and the road flies by in a second. I even manage to help my brother get there, and I am faster than him and my older sister. I pick myself up with the strength of my arms, and I am the last to climb up because I am careful and no one is criticizing me. And with my great strength, I pull up the ladder and don't just let it fall in a manner that might raise suspicion. Instead, I hide it on a special shelf in the barn so that whoever enters cannot see it from below. In my dream, the attic isn't darkened because there is a kind of window beside the shelf of the ladder through which we children climb up to a hidden attic filled with light and full of tasty delicacies; it's pleasant to be there, and we are calm and safe. Through the window, we can see whether the threatening men have gone away. We don't have to wait long for Mother to come with her basket to, as it were, collect apples and send us home one by one, sternly warning us to wait for a minute or two before we follow the brother or sister who left before us.

Suddenly the dream changed. It was dark all around, and all my power left me with the surrounding light and the protective company of my older brothers.

In the meantime, the spring was over, the summer and

31

fall also came and followed it, and it was winter again. The lake froze. The pure white snow on the first night had already mixed with the muddy earth to become filthy. It was difficult to travel, and the wheels of the wagons became lodged in the dirty snow; one of the wagons even capsized. Wet, freezing travelers and wagon owners came into Father's tavern, and their hot breath steamed up the windows. And we, the two daughters of the tavern owner – me, Sheindel, and my beautiful older sister, Feigaleh – were hidden from view, fearful of the drunks and hoping that no one would go wild again and overturn the tables of the tavern, break and splinter them, and threaten to destroy the family's living quarters. But in the meantime, everything is calm in the tavern, as if the cold outside has also cooled the visitors' blood, and they only want a glass of schnapps to warm themselves before continuing. They speak in quiet voices about something that happened in the town: the wheel of one of the wagons turned on its axle and made the coachman fall onto the muddy ground, and the heavy wagon itself fell on top of the unfortunate man. Despite the many people crowding around the wagon, they couldn't pick it up and save him, not even when they joined forces in their attempt. Pale, frightened, and moaning… the coachman's red blood seeped onto the mud-stained snow. Suddenly, a woman wearing a black shawl and a dark blue dress, a haggler in the market, arrived.

"You ne'er-do-well nobody, what's this? I heard that you overturned the wagon! All I need is for you to have broken something, and we'll have to put the little money we have into repairing it! And I haven't even done the shopping, and we need medicine for the little one… and why, suddenly,

32

don't you answer me? Did you also swallow your tongue?"

And as she drew closer, she suddenly saw the extent of the disaster, witnessed the coachman's blood and white face, and understood why he was silent. She leaned over him and stroked his thinning hair, bringing her head close to his, whispering words of affection to him, looking up from time to time at the people standing around, and a wail escaped her lips.

"What is this, good people? Why don't you do something? Why don't you do something to save him?"

Among the large crowd of men are some who have known the couple for years and the coachman from childhood. They grew up together, quarreled with one another, and together they boasted about their strength and chased the girls — but now it seems that the wagon is too heavy, and even when they join forces, they can't move it.

And the woman is silent. Leaning on all fours, she bends down over the man lying in the snow, embraces his neck in both hands and rests her head on his chest. And he tries to smile at her.

Suddenly two young Jews approach. One of them is tall and well built; he takes off his coat and hands it to his friend, rolls up his sleeves, and on his own, without any help, picks up the wagon and directs the flabbergasted observers to pull the injured coachman out from under the wheels very carefully.

"The Jew" is what everyone calls him. "Yes, The Jew." They turn to my father, "He's one of yours! He said his name is Jacob Isaac."

When Father went to pray at the synagogue, he heard more details about the two young Jews, particularly the one who saved the coachman. It turned out that both of them were students of Rabbi Arieh Leib Halperin. The hero, Jacob Isaac, was strong indeed, not only in his physical prowess but also in his knowledge from books; he was a brilliant student of great stature.

Father immediately decided to hire the services of the hero to teach my young brothers. Of course he also thought it would not hurt if Jacob Isaac were nearby if the drunkards rioted.

MATIL'S VISIT

Four Jewish Brides.

The four of them are dressed in white. Four beautiful young brides. Four smiling, laughing brides. A soft light illuminates them.

Two of them stand, the third is seated, and the fourth leans over her. They are preoccupied with themselves and unaware of what is happening around them. Their white clothes are no more than shrouds. White shrouds, some of which have crumbled. The four form a circle and start dancing, and their movements resemble floating. The two sisters, Sheindel and Breindel-Feigaleh, enter the circle. And Sheindel says, "Listen, and I'll tell you the story of Feigaleh and her *tzadik*, The Jew."

And so, Sheindel tells the story.

When Feigaleh reached the age of sixteen, it was decided to marry her off. They looked for a suitable match, but Feigaleh found fault with every candidate who sought her hand. One was short-sighted, the other was too short, and the third was too tall. He giggles at every nonsensical thing; the other is so gloomy that the whole year is one long day of mourning the destruction of the Temple. They had almost given up hope on the choosy young woman, but then Matil – the mother of Jacob Isaac, my brothers' teacher – arrived.

We learned years later that Jacob Isaac initiated his mother's arrival at our house. Jacob Isaac was spoken of favorably, but just like Feigaleh, he had rejected all the proposed matches. His mother understood from his hints that something was happening, and she decided to visit him in Apt. She was a small, energetic woman, and it was clear that she knew how to read a situation. When she came into our house, my sister offered her a hot cup of tea and biscuits. Matil looked the girl over and saw that she was beautiful, that her behavior was good, and that her manner was pleasant. Matil was a practical woman, so she also checked the house. She checked out the pots on the stove and curiously examined the two shelves in the kitchen, one for milk products with cream, cheese, and butter, and the other for meat products, with salted chicken pieces lying on it. She checked the silverware in the cabinet, kiddush cups, Elijah the Prophet's tall, decorated goblet, the impressive etrog (citron) box, and boxes of snuff to sniff. And Matil was especially impressed with the bookshelf beside the crockery cupboard. From what she could discern, this was a house of plenty, and she decided to accept her son's initiative and speak favorably of Feigaleh's qualities as a potential bride for him.

She turned to Mother and said, "I am pleased that Jacob Isaac is staying with you. I worried about him, so I decided to see where he lived. I never understood why he decided to leave our home in Przedbórz. People also study Torah there. There are so many students there that they call the city "Miniature Israel" or "Little Israel," but my Jacob Isaac decided to come here to Apt, of all places, to follow his rabbi, Arieh Leib Halperin. He is a brilliant student who doesn't take care of himself. Even as a child, he loved helping his fellow man, distributing the good food I prepared to the poor children. He was accustomed to comfort in our house. My husband, Rabbi Asher, serves as the Head of the Rabbinical Court in the town, and thank God we are well provided for. But I worry when my son is away from home. Indeed, he did come here with his friend Yeshaya, but you know how it is… Now I am calmer, knowing that he is at your house and that you watch out for him."

Mother, who hadn't understood Jacob Isaac, kept silent. Matil mistook her silence for agreement, but since she knows that her son never revealed his nature to others, she continued telling his story.

"You know, my son hides his deep knowledge of the Torah. In his childhood, his father – my husband, Rabbi Asher – got angry with him sometimes because he would not pray out loud and sway back and forth like the other boys and because instead of sitting in the Beit Hamidrash (the study hall), he would go out and study nature in the trees, flowers, and animals in the forest. But once Asher heard Jacob Isaac praying out loud with passion and enthusiasm on his own in the old synagogue in our town… Our ancient synagogue is breathtakingly beautiful, made entirely of burnished wood, and large chandeliers illuminate it with precious light. At any rate, from then on, Asher stopped scolding the boy. He understood that he has what it takes…"

And Matil continued telling her story.

"Once, my husband's brother visited us, and the three of them went to the sheep's pen to check on the flock. Suddenly, the sheep started fighting over the food they were given. Young Jacob Isaac approached them, soothed them with his soft voice, stroked the lambs, and divided the food equally among them. His uncle foresaw then that the boy was destined to become a leader, since this is how many leaders begin their journeys – as shepherds… 'When this boy grows up,' he said, 'he'll be like Abraham, Isaac and Jacob, Moses and David…' And by the way, I must tell you that my husband's brother, a man of stature, is reputed to be one of the 36 hidden righteous men who sustain the world in their generation."

When Matil saw that Mother's face had softened, she decided to speak about the matter that had brought her to Apt:

"Madame Golda, I see that you have a daughter who has come of age, and my son, Jacob Isaac, serves here as a teacher. I don't doubt that had you not become acquainted with his advantages, you would not have taken him into your home to teach your young and impressionable sons. As one mother to another, I can tell you: There is no bridegroom better suited to your Feigaleh than my son! There are none smarter than he, and he is a great hero who loves his fellowman. I know he will go far. He will not remain a teacher forever. He will be a great rabbi, and his name will be remembered for generations…"

Mother hesitated and decided not to answer immediately, but to seek my father's advice. She told Matil, "I can't decide on such a matter on my own… Let's call her over and ask her opinion."

To Mother's amazement, Feigaleh immediately agreed to marry Jacob Isaac, and the date for their marriage was set for spring. How beautiful the wedding was! My mother busied herself for a fortnight preparing for it. Many guests were invited to the joyous occasion, and on arrival they had the good luck to taste her delicacies: gefilte fish (stuffed fish), chicken, and goose, sweet carrot tzimmes (stew) with raisins, sweet sponge cake, honey wafers… and neither did Father hold back. He served the best drinks from the tavern for the honored guests and the beggars, who were also honored. The musicians entertained the guests with their melodies, and when Feigaleh and Jacob Isaac stood under the marriage canopy, the bridegroom did not attempt to hide his love. He looked at her with open admiration, and she looked down, but her smile gave away her great joy.

See how beautiful my older sister is: her flowing hair, warm brown eyes, straight nose, pink lips, and rounded chin. Her full brows were painted on her forehead as if by an artist. A few days before the wedding, when Feigaleh tried on her ivory-colored wedding dress and her braid lay on her shoulder, I looked at her through the window and saw how the wind was blowing fiercely, and the color of the clouds was the color of her dress. There was a dreamy look on my sister Feigaleh's face. She looked as if she had been taken from a portrait painted by John Singer Sargent as a "Tribute to Edouard Manet," painted as a beautiful, gentle girl sitting on a rock by the banks of a stream, the yellow of the flowers in the water reflected in her dress; her fingers are long, and her neck is also long, so that the slight deformity of her lips is almost invisible: her lower lip is not parallel to her upper one but droops slightly on one side and always gives her a unique look as if she is wondering about the incomprehensible, arbitrary world. The black stream in the painting did not predict good things to come, either.

THE FOREST RANGER

And Sheindel continues her story:

After their marriage, Feigaleh and Jacob Isaac would dine at Father's table and eat all their meals at our home. The whole family would sit together and discuss current affairs. Those were good days and pleasant hours. One day, Jacob Isaac said that our custom of lengthening meal times with conversation did not appeal to him since it made him waste valuable time when he should be studying Torah.

Jacob Isaac's words scalded Mother's heart. She snarled at Father, "I don't like the character of our son-in-law... he is an enigma to me. He is always welcoming, kind, cordial, and honest, yet he doesn't want to sit with us for meals because he thinks they take too long. Is our conversation stupid and useless? How can conversation with family members be a waste of time?"

She bowed to Jacob Isaac's will for lack of choice. Still, she firmly refused to forego her daily meeting with her daughter. She insisted on Feigaleh coming to our house daily to take the midday meal and food to prepare their evening meal and breakfast for the following day.

After a few weeks, rumors revealed that Jacob Isaac did not dine with Feigaleh but wrapped up his serving and took it immediately to the Beit Hamidrash, where he shared most of his meal with the poor. Jacob Isaac and his friends sit there together with the poor of the village and eat the best of my mother's cuisine!

There were other things that Jacob Isaac did that my mother and father were not enthusiastic about. Indeed, he continued studying Torah, as they expected of him, but rejected all their pleas that he should travel to study with Rabbi Avraham Yehoshua Heshel; they also found his prayer customs extremely strange. Instead of rising early in the morning and praying in a minyan of ten men,[6] he would pray when he felt like it, and when my father asked him about it, he replied, "I only pray when I feel ready."

"There are customs affecting prayer that you certainly are familiar with, like when to pray and with whom," Father replied, bewildered and shocked.

"That's right," Jacob Isaac replied, "but what does it resemble? It's like soldiers in the army. According to the book, they teach them all the rules: when to run, when to walk slowly, how to hold a weapon, how to fire, and how to behave in a battle. All that is well and good in quiet times of peace. In times of war, soldiers cannot behave according to the rules they learn when there is peace. In wartime, each man must save himself and his friends from the enemy, even if he cannot stand and treat his wounds, because if he does so, he or his friend could be killed. So, that is why they hurry and run, even if they don't do so according to the rule that they must walk. So, it is with prayer. The customs of prayer are valid in times of peace. But I, when I pray, I am at

---

6. Most Jewish prayer requires a minyan, or a quorum of ten adult men, although some prayers can be recited with fewer.

war, and in order not to endanger myself in this war, to save my soul and all the other souls, I am obliged to do things differently."

My father didn't understand what his son-in-law was talking about and, what's more, he rarely saw Jacob Isaac praying, neither walking or on the run. And he didn't know that Jacob Isaac prayed in that same attic where we, the children, had hidden away from the drunks. He would prepare himself for prayer for a long time and only begin when he felt spiritually ready. His strange movements when praying were so weird that he preferred to pray in the barn full of hay, straw, and food for the horses and the people who came to stay at the tavern. No one knew where he prayed other than Feigaleh, the wife of his youth. She knew, and he asked her to watch over him and examine him after the prayer because he would often lose consciousness in the intensity of his enthusiasm. Then Feigaleh would climb up to his hiding place and very gently wake him, until he regained consciousness; then they would immediately leave the barn, one after the other, and go into the house. Feigaleh would prepare a cup of hot tea for him and add a dry bagel to restore his soul.

Once, Rabbi Avraham Yehoshua Heshel, the same Hassidic leader my father wanted Jacob Isaac to study with, passed by the house when he detected a pleasant fragrance coming from the barn. He sent his manservant to check out who was home. He returned and said that he didn't see anyone. The rabbi decided to examine the matter himself. Jacob Isaac, who noticed his arrival, came down from the attic and begged Rabbi Heshel not to reveal his secret to anyone. The rabbi acceded to Jacob Isaac's wish, and thus my father continued believing that his son-in-law was shirking prayer.

Moreover, a rumor reached my father's ear that his son-in-law, Jacob Isaac, did not join the rest of the students when they bathed in the ritual bath. The Jews in Apt would bathe in an icy stream up the mountain. It was very deep, freezing, and always covered by a thin layer of ice. Because of their fear of heights and the cold, the students would climb the mountain to bathe in a group of ten or more, and when they reached the stream, panting from the climb up the steep mountain, they would light a bonfire to warm themselves after immersing. But Jacob Isaac never joined them, so when Father heard this, it sparked his rage, so he decided that he who distributes the food to the poor for which he works so hard, neither prays nor even bathes – would be wise to make a living on his own.

Who was angry with Jacob Isaac? My father or my mother? I knew how much my mother loved Jacob Isaac and in what high respect and esteem she held him. Everyone knew that – demonstrated by the marital bed she prepared for my sister, and her prayer that I, too, would be granted a bridegroom like him. But see how they blame the women for anything that lacks justice or grace? Even Martin Buber, of blessed memory, fell into the trap of Hassidic hatred toward women since, according to him, my father did not manage the tavern. According to his version, it was my mother who ran it, examined every man entering the bar, and with one glance could immediately assess his worth; it was she, of all people, who could not correctly appraise Jacob Isaac, and therefore began to bear him a grudge. When she learned that her fine cuisine was being handed out to total strangers, to ne'er-do-wells who could not make a living, she got angry and persuaded my father to stop giving them supplies and sharing their meals.

My mother, according to Buber, was to blame for starving Jacob Isaac and her beloved daughter...

But Mother was not at fault; it was Father. He rushed to judge rumors and did not know that each night before dawn, Jacob Isaac would go alone and immerse himself in the freezing stream, high up in the mountain, at an hour when darkness still covered the world, and the trees, so black and tall, were alternately hidden and revealed by the light of the lamp that his son-in-law held in his hand to illuminate the path that got higher and higher. And each day, Jacob Isaac would ascend the mountain a little earlier than the day before. And why did he make it earlier? Because Jacob Isaac and Feigaleh's room faced the blacksmith's workshop, and at the hour when Jacob Isaac and Feigaleh went to bed, the blows of the blacksmith's hammer were still being heard.

The blacksmith also rose before dawn, and Jacob Isaac said to himself, "If the blacksmith gets up earlier every day and his work is to serve this world, it is fitting that I awaken earlier to do the Creator's work for the next world."

And thus, according to the example of the industrious blacksmith, Jacob Isaac would extend his learning until the late hours of the night and wake earlier to climb the mountain, bathe in the mikveh,[7] and prepare himself for prayer. Still, each time he awakened, he found that the blacksmith had risen even earlier and was already awake and sitting at his anvil.

---

7. A bath used for ritual immersion in Judaism to achieve purity.

And our Jacob Isaac did not know that the blacksmith would study him, our Jew, through the window of the blacksmith's shop, and tell himself that if that Jew was already awake, it must be late, so he tried to wake up even earlier the following morning. And this is how it came about that both of them, as one, were getting up just a little after midnight to go to their work – one to his day's work, and the other to God's work.

The Jew later said that it was only thanks to the blacksmith that he learned how to worship God, and because of him he learned how to climb the sacred, celestial stairs step by step – because Jacob Isaac never stood on the same level of worship and was always ascending the celestial spheres, like a man who comes upon the face of the king sitting on the top floor of his palace and must go through many strange rooms and halls and many tangled stairways and almost lose his way in the convoluted corridors trying to get there if he wants to lower his gaze in respect at the foot of the king's throne. The road is not easy, and it is difficult to succeed; even one who knows how to climb from sphere to sphere does not always have the strength to reach the target and the throne itself, but has no choice but to try and climb, step by step, each day anew.

Each night at midnight, Jacob Isaac would go up the mountain alone, without another soul. The wind would blow hard, making the flame in the lantern flicker and dance as it got smaller, until it was almost extinguished. But at that moment, Jacob Isaac – his thin coattails fluttering in the wind – remembers to cover the lantern with the palms of his hands to protect the flame, which recovers, grows brighter and higher, and illuminates his way in the dark night. And he climbs up the mountain, carefully placing one foot after the other so as not to trip and fall in the dense forest. He doesn't light a bonfire to warm himself when he reaches the stream. He only immerses himself in the freezing water and hurries home immediately afterward, where he studies secretly for a few hours and, before dawn, gets into bed to warm himself a little.

"When he enters the Beit Hamidrash, it is already bustling and full of students learning, while he, Jacob Isaac, appears to have just woken up since none of his fellow students know about his nightly immersions. Essentially, only two women know: Feigaleh, his wife, and a woman who dwelt in a poor hut on the pathway leading up to the stream. The woman baked cakes for a living and had a husband, a forest keeper, heavy-bodied and tall, whom she loved with all her heart and soul. There were few tall men in the village, and her forest keeper was taller and more robust than everyone else – and with that, he was sensitive and gentle, had a good voice, and would sing her love songs. The forest belonged to a landowner, and the trees were his property, so only his men could fell them. And as the trees were tall and heavy, they would transport them on the river.

Once, robbers entered the forest and chopped down a tree at night, and the woman's husband, who lived in the woods, got up and went to them. She begged him to stay home because they could hear that there were many robbers, and it was understandable that despite his strength, he would not be able to defeat all of them. But he was insistent and hushed her, saying he had no intention of abusing the landowner's trust. He made her swear not to leave the house and follow him, no matter what awful noises she might hear; he also gave her a sign that if he returned – that's what he said, "*If* I return," not "*When* I return" – he'll knock hard three times and follow with two softer ones – then she should open the door for him. But if that didn't happen, she must not unbolt the door under any circumstances. So when the forest keeper went out, his wife heard his footsteps as he walked away, followed by a sudden silence. In that silence, she listened to the sound of running feet, and there was no knocking at the door. When the morning came, she went outside to the place from where the voices were heard, and there, in a small clearing, she saw a felled tree and a man soaking in blood. The tree had not been taken, but with the blows of an axe, they had taken the love of her life. Her loud, bitter cry was heard as it echoed through the trees.

She asked to remain in the small hut, and the landlord yielded after she promised to take care of the forest instead of her beloved; she also promised that every time she heard thieves in the forest, she would leave the house secretly to call the police. The landowner had no choice but to accept her offer since no one was in a rush to replace the murdered watchman.

One night, before dawn, the forest guard's widow heard light footsteps and saw a man walking while holding a lighted lantern. The wind played with the tails of his coat, and she didn't suspect that he had come to fell trees because he didn't have an axe; he carried only a white shirt and a white towel around his neck, and wore a light coat on his body that fluttered in the wind. He hummed a gentle melody, and his voice was quiet as if he didn't want to disturb the forest's nap. The image of the stranger walking alone in the woods reminded her of her murdered beloved, and she decided to follow him and see where he was going. And here, close to the top of the mountain, where the stream had created a small pool, the man took off his clothes, folded them carefully, and laid the white towel on top of them. He was tall and well-built, and his white body resembled that of her late beloved's. The woman wanted to embrace the singing stranger, but she continued hiding and watching him immerse himself in the pool. He stood in the water with his legs apart like a man with a hoe, raised his arms like one picking fruit off a tree, recited a few words aloud in an unfamiliar language, and entirely submerged himself into the water until it covered his head. Worried that he might not reemerge, she almost came out of her hiding place. Then his head appeared, and she feared that the stranger heard her sigh of relief. And three more times, the water covered him completely – the woman, of course, did not know that he'd immersed himself twice to cast out the spirit of impurity and receive the spirit of purity, and two more times because he intended to delve into the Holy Kabbalah.[8] When he emerged from the water with nimble steps, he wiped his body with the towel, and light illuminated his forehead. It seemed to her that a saint or an angel was standing before her, and she could no longer stand the beauty of his appearance and revealed herself to him; his eyes saw hers, and as his teeth chattered from the intense cold, he slowly dried himself and put on his clothes.

She didn't know if he would come again the following night, but he did come, climbed up the mountain, and she walked behind him without attempting to hide and with-

---

8. Kabbalah is an esoteric method, discipline, and school of thought in Jewish mysticism.

out saying a word. She was tall and willowy. Although the darkness prevented him from seeing her face, he only saw that she bore a pile of twigs on her back, but he knew that her intentions were good and did not fear her – and even smiled a bit when he saw the twigs. And when he was immersed in the water, deep in thought, she gathered the white towel and his clothes and placed them close to the fire she lit with the twigs so that when he emerged from the frozen water they would warm him. On the third night, when Jacob Isaac went to the pool, the fire was already burning in a small tin barrel, and the tall woman – whose face was now visible, as were the tears welling up in her eyes, in the patch of light the fire spread around – stood a distance away and adjusted the green shawl on her shoulders. And so she stood and watched him every night, sure that her beloved husband had sent him to her from the heavens. She knew that if he approached her, she would give herself to him, but he never did; she also knew that if she approached him, perhaps he would stop coming and she would never see him again. And so she never again left the shadows that the fire she lit in the barrel cast on the trees.

If Father had known how things were, perhaps he would have been kinder to Jacob Isaac and not as angry as he was with him. But Father remained ignorant and was furious that Jacob Isaac was not studying properly, nor was he praying correctly or immersing himself as he should – it was very doubtful that he was a brilliant Torah student as promised – and he did nothing to make a living for his daughter and grandchildren. He spends his days tucked away in his room, feasting with the town's poor on the delicacies that his wife sends him, or else he wanders around among the tall trees on the hills close to Apt, gazing at the headstones in the old cemetery and doesn't even join the others in prayer.

And Father was so angry with his son-in-law that he turned to him with harsh words.

"Listen here, my boy," he addressed him in a tone intended to belittle him. "I indeed undertook to support you and your family, but no more, even though I can do so. But you spend your days wandering around the woods, and although you sit in the synagogue with your friends and among the town beggars, you do not devote your time to study. It seems that you are not the scholar I wished for, and when I give you or my daughter food and money that should suffice to keep you for a few days, the following day, my daughter comes to ask for more because of your decision not allow a zloty or even a grosz to remain overnight in your home. It kills me even to try to understand this."

"I will explain it to you," said Jacob Isaac. "There are so many children who don't have even a crumb to eat for supper. And I see no reason to leave any money, a grosz or a zloty overnight in my house when it can do so much good. That is why I go to the market to give every leftover coin in my possession to someone with nothing to feed his children. And I am certain that you can understand that."

"Of course I can understand," my father calmly replied, "but you also have to understand something, and that is that I undertook to provide for my daughter, for you, and for your children. If you want to help anyone in need of food, I have no problem with that, but to do that, you must first leave my home and work for your living."

Feigaleh and Jacob Isaac left our father's house and

moved into a shabby room close to the synagogue. Thus poverty entered their home. In those days, many already valued The Jew for his sharp intellect and appointed him to head the Apt Rabbinical Court. Nevertheless, both he and Feigaleh were thin and pale. It was known that Jacob Isaac thought about their situation and concluded that it was sufficient for a man to have only a little to eat. As for himself, he would even forego that if he didn't require the food to have enough strength to teach his students and talk to them. And so he and Feigaleh began to lose weight, even though they could have made a decent living. But you should know that no matter how high his position, how much he was paid, how many his followers numbered, or how rich the people who supported them were, he always gave everything he had and made do with the least of the least. He did so on principle. Remember that because – for better or for worse – The Jew was a man of principles, and one of his principles determined that the soul or the spirit is much more important than the body. Therefore, to ascend, he would climb up to the Apt pool to isolate himself in its forests and on the hill beside the old cemetery and pray in complete secrecy.

And that same woman – the forest guard who lived alone in her hut – took pains to keep him warm and knew that he was a remarkable man. The storytellers accused her – of all people! – of breaking his trust and revealing the secret of his greatness to all. And they found fault with her, the unfortunate widow whose husband was murdered, and in whose memory she did whatever she could to help The Jew. And like all the women who surrounded The Jew, her role was also to reveal the holiness of Jacob Isaac through her faults.

THE DEATH OF A BELOVED BIRD

And Sheindel continues her story:

When his spiritual virtue became known to the residents of Apt, Jacob Isaac understood that he had nothing more to seek in our little town. He was also terrified of committing the sin of pride and was just uncomfortable at being considered superior to everyone else. So The Jew began combing the streets of neighboring villages and became a teacher of very young children. The couple faced difficult days, as they were already raising three children. And while Jacob Isaac was on the road, Feigaleh sat alone at home.

Jacob Isaac regarded these difficulties as an experience he had to live through, a test of his being a Jew, because each day he saw himself as one who might stop being a Jew and become a gentile. He was a robust man, and despite growing weaker, he managed to keep his strength and even grew stronger spiritually. He also acquired new friends on the roads; among them was Rabbi David of Lelov, and they grew very close. I loved Rabbi David. He had a great soul and was always compassionate toward his fellowman; he even had mercy on animals. It was once told that on Rosh Hashana, when they intended to blow the *shofar* (the ram's horn), Rabbi David was not in the synagogue; they found him outside, feeding barley to the horses from a huge skullcap he used to wear. The cart owner had hurried to hear the shofar and left his hungry horses waiting for him. Rabbi David saw their plight and fed them himself, and it was said that by his act of kindness, the shofar-blowing succeeded in opening the Gates of Heaven.

Indeed, The Jew preserved his physical and spiritual resilience despite poverty and starvation. Still, Feigaleh, who, unlike him, also suffered from loneliness, was becoming weaker. Her face became sallow, her body withered, and with the intense cold that prevailed that winter, she fell ill, and severe coughing attacks were frequently heard in their home. Despite everything, she remained as beautiful as ever. My beloved sister was only twenty-one and in the prime of her life on the terrible day that she died. She left behind three children: Yerachmiel, Rivka Rachel, and the chuckling baby whom I loved the most, Sarah Leah, named for her older sister, and recalled the names of the "Four Mothers" of the nation. I was ten years old when Feigaleh was gathered unto her mothers, and I could not but blame Jacob Isaac for the death of my beloved, beautiful sister. I loved her, and all who were privileged to know her did, too. I was furious. I couldn't help believing that had Jacob Isaac not decided that there was no need to take care of the physical being, she would not have grown so weak and might still be among the living. I was also angry with my father because when he punished Jacob Isaac for dispersing the wealth that he had, he punished my sister Feigaleh, so I felt that he, too, had a part in her death. After Feigaleh's passing – Feigaleh, my beloved bird – her children stayed in our home, and my mother raised them.

Jacob Isaac continued going around the small towns and villages teaching Torah, but, as life happens, he regularly visited his children and came into our house more often than he did during Feigaleh's lifetime. I would listen to the bedtime stories he told five-year-old Yerachmiel, stories of wonders that he beheld on his wanderings, of fabulous animals like the "*tachash*," an animal that was specially bred for the building of the Temple, a beautiful colorful creature with a single horn on its forehead. And I suppose it seems that the Christians invented the unicorn because you first came across it in children's coloring books on your travels to one of the countries overseas. In that case, you should know that he also originates with us although, unlike the unicorn known to the gentiles, our tachash is not white, and its skin has myriad shades: azure and blue, pink and purple, rose and scarlet, yellow and crimson.

Like Yerachmiel, I loved the tachash and Jacob Isaac's stories and the tunes he sang to little Yerachmiel. These songs bore him to upper worlds, and just like Chinghiz Aytmatov, the Kyrgyzi author whose works you love so much, I felt that the melody itself, in its interior, was no less than a kind of pilgrimage of the soul to the galaxy of the spirit, to the language of the universe, to God. I felt that Jacob Isaac's melodies made me fly above the clouds and rise high above them until I was liberated.

With the passing of the years, his melodies made it impossible for me not to fall hopelessly in love with him, like that beautiful Jamila, who loved her Daniyar to desperation because of the songs he sang to her in the glades of Kyrgyz.

Yerachmiel also learned his father's tunes, and he worked to the sound of them. More than once, when I missed his father, I would hide behind the alcove where he fixed the clocks and listened to his songs. But that was years later . . . so let's not get ahead of ourselves.

BETWEEN PRAYER AND LOVE

Four Jewish Brides.

The four of them are dressed in white. Four beautiful young brides. Four smiling, laughing brides. A soft light illuminates them.

Two of them stand, the third is seated, and the fourth leans over her. They are preoccupied with themselves and unaware of what is happening around them. Their white clothes are no more than shrouds. White shrouds, some of them have crumbled. The four form a circle and start dancing, and their movements resemble floating.

Sheindel enters the circle again – alone, this time – and she turns to me and says, "I, Sheindel, will tell you the story of my marriage."

And so Sheindel told me:

After Feigaleh died, I was supposed to get married to him, to The Jew. Indeed, it must seem strange to you that a sister would marry her sister's widower. It isn't accepted in your generation, but it is explicit in the tractates of the Talmud. It isn't acceptable to marry the sister of your wife if your wife is still alive since it is unseemly to turn two sisters into competitive wives, not only in the sense of enemies but also in the sense of two women envying one another because he may overlook her needs when he is with the other one. But all that applies only if both sisters are alive. As opposed to that, a widower left with small children is permitted to remarry immediately without waiting a year because the children must be cared for.

It is told that when the wife of Joseph the Priest of the Second Temple died, he asked her sister at the cemetery, "Go take care of your sister's children. Go into my house, marry me, and raise your sister's children."

But I was only ten years old when Feigaleh died, and Jacob Isaac acceded to my mother's request to delay the wedding until I reached puberty; my mother promised that she would take care of the children until then.

In those days, Jacob Isaac would travel frequently. He would stay at our house for a few days, and after Shabbat he would hurry to set out on his travels and go on his way. In those days, he wandered around the various Polish villages. He deepened his friendship with Rabbi David of Lelov, the Rabbi David who had stood in our father's tavern yard and insisted that the wagon owners feed the horses before they started eating. In those days, Jacob Isaac became acquainted with The Preacher of Kozhnitz, a weak man who spent all his days in a bed covered with furs to keep warm. When it was time to pray, he would be carried to the synagogue by his followers, but the moment he entered the holy place, he would jump to his feet, pray with enormous verve, and speak in a thunderous voice that terrified all who heard him.

And Rabbi David introduced Jacob Isaac to Simcha Bunim; the two would sit together and hold long conversations into the night. They became incredibly close after my father chased Feigaleh and Jacob Isaac out of his house, and the two left Apt with their children and moved to the village of Peshischa. In the evenings they would sit and talk, and Simcha Bunim talked about himself. He was educated and close to the intellectuals, who felt that the traditions handed down from previous generations were not enough for them. They also wanted to study the great philosophers and delve into the sciences. Like them, Simcha Bunim would wear short, tailored suits and a hat, see plays in theaters, and play card games in nightclubs. He earned his living managing the Bergson family's timber business, and he handled the transportation of the felled logs on rafts along the rivers of Poland to the city of Danzig. Later, when he felt science pulling at his heart, Simcha Bunim invested his money in studying pharmacology. When he earned his diploma and license, he was awarded a monetary prize for his conscientiousness, enough to buy a professional text, but he decided to spend it on a copy of the Zohar.[9] In the end, with the assistance of his employer, Temerl Bergson, the "Doña Gracia of Hassidism," he opened a pharmacy in Peshischa. Simcha Bunim was a polyglot who spoke four foreign languages fluently – Latin, German, Polish, and Russian.

Jacob Isaac and Simcha Bunim held similar opinions. They were both learned and beloved, brilliant scholars, and they both hated and ridiculed the tricks and miracles performed by the "tzadikim"[10] and "Masters of the Good Name"[11] who used magia for healing. They both claimed that

---

9. The Zohar is a foundational work in the literature of Jewish mystical thought known as Kabbalah.

10. Plural, in Hebrew, for tzadik.

11. In Hebrew, *Baal Shem* - or "Master of the Good Name" - is a term for a healer who wields the secret name of God.

miracles are contrary to the natural order and that their effect is temporary and fleeting. They believed that daily acts of kindness have a much more significant and lasting impact on the world order. They concluded that every Hassid is responsible for himself and serving his God rather than relying on the miracles of the tzadikim. They both thought that each Hassid has to find the right path for himself, to protect himself from fruitless imitation of the way of the tzadikim that doesn't always suit him and his nature. Simcha Bunim even used to say that every man has to choose his way of serving God – with seriousness, as in Ecclesiastes, or out of joy, as in the Song of Songs. He held that the Hassid has to follow both paths simultaneously, which means on the one hand, be modest and humble in his approach to God, believe that he is worthless and insignificant – literally, no more than dust and ashes like Ecclesiastes. At the same time, he should take the approach of "the world was created for me" and not run away from its pleasures and joy; no one way is preferred. The right way, Simcha Bunim held, is to combine both, like King Solomon did when he wrote both Ecclesiastes and The Song of Songs. Bunim taught that both ways make it possible to raise sacred sparks and influence the correction of the spheres and the supernal worlds. Indeed, Simcha Bunim admitted that King Solomon chose to live his daily life along the path of The Song of Songs because of his sympathetic attitude to physicality and sensual pleasures. And, honestly, Simcha Bunim was also inclined to do so. He explained that on the Sabbath, it was appropriate to relax and recline on velvet sofas, study a little Torah, and whoever wishes, may sleep a little, eat roast meat and drink wine, then learn a bit more Torah, and that this is the intention of an "additional soul" we receive on Shabbat so that we are able to reach a higher level of the spirit and not feel locked up and closed off on that day. Eating good foods serves as a tool to rectify and correct the foods that may have been reincarnated by a spirit looking to be corrected.

So Simcha Bunim loved life and would indulge his family with a life of well-being in beautiful clothes and jewels. His wife always flaunted her attire, yet was well-read, wise, intelligent, and an excellent helpmate. In this regard, his approach was similar to that of The Seer of Lublin, who also connected the world of love in the Song of Songs to the role of the righteous leader in taking care of the physical well-being of his disciples. For him, too, this role involved ensuring a life of well-being suitable for the righteous leader himself.

As opposed to them, my Jacob Isaac preferred the severe and modest approach of Ecclesiastes to the sensuous and pleasured style of the Song of Songs. Still, despite their differing individual approaches, Simcha Bunim and The Jew shared a good friendship. Simcha, a man of the big world, was involved in the material realm as a person in commerce and a pharmacist. His familiarity with that world allowed him to see its shallowness, and he decided to turn his life around and fully repent.

He told Jacob Isaac that when he was a merchant in Danzig, he negotiated with one of the farmers, who asked him to add to the price he offered. When he got home and thought about the farmer's words, he understood that they contained a secret, and he had to add to his offer as part of his service to God and to make complete repentance.

"My life as a modern intellectual," Simcha Bunim told his friend, "taught me how people sin, what their sins are, what tempts them, and what the root of sin is. I know what the sickness of the generation is. After all, since I am a pharmacist, the jars of medicinal drugs in my pharmacy contain cures for all the causes of sin," he said; when he saw that Jacob Isaac furrowed his brow as if he didn't understand, he continued and explained:

"It is best to receive reprimands and admonitions from those who understand the way of fools and clowns, who appreciate their songs and temptations because that way they can compose their words of criticism most effectively."

But the main matters of concern to Jacob Isaac and his friends were in the upper spheres. They knew that before God created the world, he condensed himself, emptying space within him since he had to make room for the world he was to create. And he placed the light that poured out of him to the world in a variety of containers or vessels, which were the spheres, except that they could not encompass and contain it. They broke, sending out sparks of light that spread over the world and everything on it – even the trees and rocks – and now man must elevate these scattered sparks of holiness again and return them to their source. That was the reason it was created. Some say that the vessels broke because the forces of evil also grew more potent in the war between light and darkness that began at the moment of creation. But I want to avoid getting into this ancient war. I am just trying to explain what happened to The Jew when he prayed. When The Jew prayed, he tried raising the dispersed sparks in the world to repair the broken vessels. To that end, he prayed with such intensity and devotion that he almost lost himself and his sense of the here and now. He was all spirit, and he neglected his corporeal manifestation and united with God.

In his prayers, The Jew reached the supernal worlds. It is said that each of the tzadikim excelled in a different aspect of righteousness. My Jew was gifted with the ability to pray. He didn't simply pray because it was the appointed time to say "*Sh'ma Yisrael*" (Hear O Israel) in the morning. He only prayed after preparing himself for it with all his might, after immersing himself secretly and alone in the mikveh, and only when his heart was filled with emotion as his soul was tensed to fly up high like an arrow from a bow, yet feeling close to the dust of the earth, like a vessel full of worthless dirt and shame, and whose soul is so hollow that it longs to surrender and be filled with spirituality. Then he speaks, whispers, and shouts the words of the prayer. Sometimes his voice trembles, and sometimes it gets completely lost in the abyss, and he becomes nothing; sometimes he lingers in the upper worlds, stamping his feet as if fighting a more potent force than himself. Then I knew I had to return him to the real world immediately. At first I was frightened to touch him and I would call out his name, but my cries were in vain, and I would hear how he called out to me in anguish:

"Help me! Save me! You promised!"

And then I would draw closer to him, grab him by the arms and embrace him with considerable force because he was shaking so hard that his teeth rattled and it wasn't easy to hold him. He was cold and refused to release the prayer book in his hand until he gradually grew limp. His entire body would be scrunched up, and my hefty, gigantic hero would almost have fallen on the floor; I continued to hold him, and together we slid down on the cold floor. Beads of perspiration dripped from his black hair, and when he returned to himself at long last, he would open his green eyes and look at me with a glassy stare as if he didn't know me. I would continue holding him until he looked into my eyes, focused his gaze, calmed down, and began making love to me. Softly, gently, and I – despite the late hour of the morning and all the housework that awaited me – would surrender to his fingers and the pleasure he gave me. Once, when he cradled me in his arms, he told me, "I saw the holy sparks of Godliness in your brown eyes. I found the Godly source in you."

When Feigaleh repeated his words to me, she was already very ill and on her sickbed. She sensed that I would understand part of what she told me – but not all of it – yet she prepared me for my marriage to her husband because like me, him, and everyone, she, Feigaleh, also knew that my fate was tied to his from the day I prepared her marriage bed with our mother, and mother prayed that I would also have such a husband. After all, that prayer had immediately caused Jacob Isaac to cry bitterly because he said, "It will be my fate that this will come true." That was what he saw in the heavens.

"Each time Yitzchakele prays," my sister would instruct me, "be attentive, little Sheindeleh. Stand outside the door, listen carefully, and go to his aid as I did when he cannot revive himself."

And that is what I did. Each time Jacob Isaac prayed and lost himself in the higher heavenly spheres, I felt that I had to hurry to help him back. I called his name and held him in my arms. He looked at me, always searching for Feigaleh's brown eyes and finding only my gray ones, with no sparks of Godliness and no Divine source. He did not make love to me and only asked for a cup of tea and some dry crackers called *kichelach*. I – a damaged vessel – was a poor substitute for my sister, and he had no love for me.

When these events were repeated, and he did not seek my embrace, I would let go of him as soon as he woke up, look down, and go to the kitchen to prepare his refreshments.

SHE IS RACHEL, AND I AM LEAH

And Sheindel continues her story:

I was 12 when I married, and my bridegroom was 24 – twice my age. Pictures flashed through my mind when I prepared the wedding canopy. In my mind's eye, I recalled seeing Jacob Isaac pick up the villager's cart with his great strength and how it had amazed me, and how I rejoiced on the day he married my beautiful sister, who was such a beautiful bride with her black hair and warm brown eyes. I also recalled his beautiful eyes, admiring his bride, my sister Feigaleh. And here, on that same day, years later, two years after my beloved sister's death, I got married – the younger sister whose nose was big and who was so ugly – to my sister's husband. Again, I remembered that wedding, with its joy and jubilation, and I couldn't help but compare it to my quiet, restrained wedding, where everyone seemed to move around on their tippy toes as if they were visiting a house of mourning.

I looked at my bridegroom wearing a *kittel* for the occasion, a white linen robe, the color of a shroud, and I was filled with compassion for what had happened to him – losing a beloved wife and having to settle for her ugly sister. And when compassion overcame me for my sister, my bridegroom, and for myself, the beggars rattled their charity boxes and cried out in terrible voices:

"Charity will save you from death! Charity will save you from death!"

I was momentarily stunned. How had my wedding turned into a funeral? Only then did it hit me that they were mourning the death of my sister Feigaleh, and a heavy cloud of depression descended on me.

After the wedding, I traveled with my husband to his house in Peshischa. My mother anxiously watched the departing wagon that she had filled with gifts and food for the journey. Apt was lined with tall, silver-barked birch trees, and on my journey from Apt to Peshischa, I enjoyed looking at the birch trees along the way, their silvery trunks, and the rays of light that shone through their branches. I comforted myself by realizing that at least the scenery wasn't changing on the trip and it resembled the familiar surroundings of my home.

I noticed peasants walking on the side of the trees with their heads down, and I knew they were searching for mushrooms. I also wanted to collect mushrooms to prepare delicious soup for my man, but the wagon didn't stop at the roadside.

We had reached Peshischa and were already passing between the houses. I saw that they were made of wood and, in the newer ones that had not yet blackened, the age rings in the wood were still visible. As I stared at the village houses, I was overcome with longing for Apt and its surrounding hills. My attention was immediately drawn to the geese in the gardens. There was something pleasant and encouraging about their cackling, but that sense of well-being faded at the screeching of many crows that sounded like a portent of difficulties and adversities.

Before my marriage, my mother explained what would happen between my husband and me on our wedding night, my first night of love, which I experienced as one who, although present, was not meant to be there. Jacob Isaac fulfilled his duty — as if compelled by demons — without even looking into my eyes, and the feeling that I had usurped my sister's place began to take root in me. Now I knew it with all my senses: I was no more than a substitute for my sister, who was better than me. We were two sisters married to one man, like Rachel and Leah, who were married to Jacob, our forefather; in their case, Leah was the older and Rachel the younger, while it was the other way around with us. She was Rachel, and I was Leah. I am Leah and younger. She is beautiful, like Rachel, and I am ugly. She is Rachel, and I am Leah. Leah's eyes were weak. And my nose was big. She is beloved, and I am despised. She was the mainstay of the home, and I was just the second in line.

I am the replacement. I have stolen the place that was my sister's by right. I tricked my way into Jacob Isaac's home. And after all, a replacement is always associated with cheating. When Laban exchanged his daughters and led Leah to the wedding canopy, he cheated without Jacob's knowledge. Also, Jacob was cheating when he misled his father and stole Isaac's birthright from his brother Esau. And anyone who is cheated also pays a heavy price for what was done. My sister paid a hefty price for my replacing her.

Rachel paid for Leah's place for seven whole years, and my sister paid with her life for the position I occupied. But when Laban exchanged Rachel with Leah, Rachel knew what would happen. She gave Leah the signs she agreed upon with Jacob to help him identify her on her wedding day. They determined the signs themselves because both of them suspected what did happen in the end – that Laban would cheat them and exchange the sisters. But in the future, Rachel revealed the signs to Leah. She did it of her own volition so that the younger sister would not marry before the older one, so as to not shame her beloved older sister, who would braid her hair. And during our childhood, my sister braided my hair. She made me sit for hours in the room and didn't let me go out to the frozen river and play with my friends while she braided my hair and whispered words of admonishment to persuade me. And here I am, taking her place after cheating my way into Jacob Isaac's home; my mother is Laban, who meddled in the stewpot and messed things up – because Mother prayed on Feigaleh's wedding night that I would be wed to a bridegroom precisely like him, and the rest is known. When Jacob Isaac heard about her prayer, he wept because he knew what would come to pass.

And when she married Jacob, Leah clung to her husband, as was the custom, and regarded her man as the center of her life, loved him, and tried to build her status in their married life through the children she bore him. All her children's names are connected to her man and her relationship with him.

When Reuven[12] was born, Leah said, "Because the Lord hath looked upon my affliction; for now, my husband will

---

12. Reuven is Hebrew for 'Look: a son!' Simeon is the English for "Shimon," which in Hebrew comes from the verb "to hear." Levi is derived from the Hebrew word that means "to accompany."

love me." When the second son was born, she said, "Because the Lord hath heard that I am hated, He hath therefore given me this son also." And she called his name Simeon." And when the third son was born, she called him Levi because, she said, "Now at last my husband will become attached to me because I have borne him three sons. Therefore was his name called Levi."

And Feigaleh, my sister, like Leah, loved her husband and regarded him as the center of her life. But I am not like that. I am the second from the top; I am the replacement. I am hated, and I know it – which is why I don't consider my man the center of my life. Not yet. I don't desire him, and I am very angry with him for going off on his wanderings and leaving my beloved sister to manage on her own, and she failed at that. But then, out of anger, I understood that I was not justified in my anger because the events occurred to fulfill my mother's innocent prayer that I would take my sister's place.

As the days go by, I find that my feelings are changing and I look forward to his touch – and not out of a yearning for a child of my own. I am still young, and I don't yet long for motherhood. But I do feel pleasure in the depths of my belly when he comes into me, and I recall that I read the story of the mandrakes in *"Tz'enah Ur'enah."*[13]

At the time of the wheat harvest, Reuven, the son of Leah, found mandrakes in the field and brought them to his mother, Leah. Rachel said to Leah, "Give me some of your

---

13. *Tz'enah Ur'enah* was one of the books popular in the Jewish world before the Second World War, was written in Yiddish for women, and follows the Torah passages, including legends, midrashim, and haftarot.

son's mandrakes." Rachel promised Leah a night of love with Jacob in exchange for the mandrakes. "He will lie with you tonight in exchange for your son's mandrakes," she said.

And I wondered about those mandrakes. Are they just heavily scented purple flowers, or is there something more to them? There must be something special about them if a story in Genesis is devoted to them. Did Rachel want them so much that she was prepared to pay for them with a night of love with the man she loved in her youth? I asked about it and was told that in ancient times, mandrakes were used for their magical properties. They used them to prepare love potions and aphrodisiacs.

The flowers had a strong, unpleasant, but intoxicating aroma that dulls the senses. The roots of the mandrakes contain anesthetic substances that induce sleep, so it is essential to chew the root in moderation because it is poisonous. What was Rachel after when she asked Leah for her son's mandrakes? Did she want to be more alluring to her husband? Did she want the mandrakes as an aphrodisiac? Did she want her husband's love to be reserved for her only and not for her sister? Was it a fertility charm? After all, it was said that Rachel was barren. Some say that her pregnancy resulted from the use of mandrakes. Or did she want them as a sleeping potion to forget and dispel the pain of her jealousy of her sister, who was also her rival? It was so important to her to get the mandrakes that she agreed to give her sister a night of love with Jacob. She traded him. And Leah, having no shame in demanding what was promised to her, went out to Jacob and demanded the night of love so that some of the sages considered her a prostitute. Was she motivated by desire because she possessed the means of arousing Jacob's lust, or out of the wish to give birth to more sons and assure herself of her power and standing as the mother of sons? At any rate, her demand to be with Jacob on the evening that Reuven brought her the mandrakes led to the birth of Issachar because she traded the mandrakes for that. And I was not astonished that Leah bought a night of love with Jacob with the mandrakes. I understood her. As time passed, I was also breathless when I remembered my nights with Jacob Isaac.

She is Rachel, and I am Leah. All the time, I remembered that Rachel was Jacob's intended wife. Jacob saw her at the well, fell in love with her, worked for her father, Laban, for seven years for him to agree to their marriage, and then replaced her with Leah on the evening of the wedding. Also, my sister Feigaleh was supposed to be with Jacob Isaac, and I replaced her. Jacob loved Rachel more and never hid his preference. And I understand Leah's jealousy. My sister was not beside me for me to envy her. But I, Sheindel, felt that same jealousy. Despite being the living sister, I felt my dead sister was his beloved wife. She was Rachel, and I was Leah. He loved her. She was loved, and I was hated. She ruled her home, and I was only the second in command. I had usurped her position.

AND WE SHALL BECOME ONE FLESH

And Sheindel continues her story:

In the early days of our marriage, I felt only rage and great confusion. I was angry with Jacob Isaac and did not want him. I blamed him for the death of my beautiful sister and didn't know how to keep my distance from him. He would come home late from the Beit Midrash, and when he attempted to initiate the act of a husband with his wife, I recoiled from him and felt myself shrinking away and becoming so tense that if I did accede, my body hurt afterward. I just wanted to push him away because I thought it was not me he sought at night, but my sister. I was nothing more than a miserable substitute for her. But things change. I grew up, formed my own opinions, and came to desire my husband. I cried out to my sister in my thoughts and beseeched her to teach me to love her husband.

And I heard Feigaleh speak to me.

"How thrilled we were when I found out I was with child," she told me. "I didn't know how to tell dear Jacob Isaac I was pregnant, but I felt that he was more tender with me. He always treated me with gentleness, but when the moon was full and he knew I was menstruating, he avoided touching my hand when he came home. If I were not, I would stroke his cheek lightly when I served him his dinner, and my thumb almost touched his lips. His eyes would light up, and he would caress my hand, take hold of it, and press it to his heart. I would lose my breath and blush. Then he would take my hand and kiss it tenderly. We both waited for nightfall and went to bed earlier than usual, because on such nights our love would elevate us to heights we did not know possible. And sometimes, when he was learning at the Beit Midrash, I remembered his embraces and longed for his long fingers to touch me, to caress my body in its most intimate places, and waited for him to come home. In the first year of our marriage, he didn't go away on his own but fulfilled the Biblical commandment not to leave a young bride alone after her marriage, and I thought that was how our lives would always be. It is said that being a prisoner to your desire for your man is part of the punishment for Eve's sin of eating the forbidden fruit. But that sentence was so wondrous. My beloved never neglected to satisfy my need, even when I was pregnant.

"In the beginning," Feigaleh continued her story, "even when the moon was full, and I did not feel well and did not gently touch his cheek during our evening meal, he still took my hand and pressed it to his heart. And so, it was in the middle of the month and the following day because he already knew it even before I knew I was with child. Our nights of love became stormier than usual, and every night my body would be so feverish with desire that I would even take off my underclothes. When I got into bed, I would immediately press myself to him, let him caress my feminine source through the material of my nightdress because the touch of the rough fabric gave me indescribable pleasure until I wanted to cleave to him.

When I noticed that his breathing was becoming faster, and feared that he might spill his seed in waste, I would take off my nightdress."

She paused with her story, and suddenly I saw her image, dressed in white, looking at me.

"I am you, and you are me," she told me.

"I am me, and you are you," I replied in fright.

"But if Mother had not messed up the whole matter, you would now be at home waiting for a marriage proposal. Because of her, I am dead, and you are married to Jacob Isaac instead of me..."

"What does Mother have to do with this? What you're saying is terrible," I protested.

"Because when you arranged my wedding bed, instead of rejoicing in my happiness, our mother sighed bitterly in a quiet voice that awakened the angels and said, if only the bridegroom will also be Sheindel's."

"She didn't say this bridegroom," I insisted. "She said like this, a bridegroom like this...."

"She must have swallowed the word 'like' and said 'him.' She didn't use the word 'like' as a comparison. She didn't say a bridegroom 'like' him. She said that bridegroom. You were a little girl, fluffing up the pillows, and you didn't understand. But when you left the room, Jacob Isaac looked at Mother and screamed out loud, "Oh, Golda! What have you done? I fear your prayer will be answered!"

"He said that the prayers of the innocent are fulfilled, and he gave me a terrified look." I remembered, "and I felt bad because I didn't want to pray at the time, so I just looked at the flickering light in the room and the scattered feathers that had been released from the pillows and flew like icy snowflakes in the glow, and I looked down so he wouldn't know that I hadn't prayed."

"But he didn't direct his remarks at you; they were directed at Mother. Yet I'm the one in the dark hole. I knew that evil spirits intervened and brought about your marriage. Bad angels, or the irony of fate, or the prophecy of a simple woman that came true. And now you are married to the love of my life, and I am here and still desire him."

"But now I am married to him!" I spoke up for myself.

"That's correct, so you can repair what went wrong. Only you can repair the wrong and make the crooked straight..."

"Me? Why are you laughing so wildly? You're scaring me..."

"Open a fissure to your soul and let me enter it. Then you'll be me. I'll be you..."

"That's forbidden!" I yelled.

"It's permissible and necessary to atone for the wrongdoing. It is both

permissible and desirable," my sister insisted.

"Leave me alone. I don't want to!"

But the alien voice echoed inside me. It echoed against my will. And sometimes, when Jacob Isaac looked at me sadly, I realized that the damage had been done not only to my sister Feigaleh, but also to him. I knew that it was not me he wanted as a wife, but my sister, who was much more beautiful than I am. And sometimes, at moments like this, I wished with all my heart to hear the voice that comes into me, "I am you, and you are me. You are me, and I am you..."

And I understood that I had to obey my sister, establish contact with her, and allow her to be part of me — and in this way, rectify the damage. I called her to come and noticed the changes in the house when I created a connection with her world of the dead. Doors suddenly slammed shut. Cold drafts blew. And there were also changes within me. I felt that I wasn't the way I had been yesterday or the day before; weakness has stricken me and I walk around as if drifting between rooms.

I found one of Feigaleh's Sabbath dresses in a closet, and since then I have worn it for entire days. I also haven't taken it off at night to change to nightclothes. The dress is too short for my height, and my ankles are bare and reveal white socks and heavy dark shoes. Jacob Isaac stares at me. His forehead creases, and a deep line arises at the junction of his forehead and nose. At dinner time, he comes into the kitchen, picks up the lids of the pots, and sees that they are empty. He slices bread and onion that he brought from the market and invites me to sit and dine with him. I chew and chew and cannot swallow the food. I feel my throat tingling and strange sounds coming out of it. If I don't remove the sticky paste from my mouth, I will choke, and when I do so, I see Jacob Isaac's shocked expression. I try to explain, but the words come out of my dark, clumsy, heavy mouth, and I can't pronounce them correctly. The consonants alternate with one another.

"I can't lowswal," I say. "It's kingcho me."

I fall asleep on the chair and wake up in the morning in the same dress and with the same sense of confusion, not knowing how I got there. I try to remember what happened the day before, but the day seems to have been erased from my memory. Entire days are wiped out. My hands itch, and when I look at them, I discover that I have scratched them until they bled.

I don't understand how the day went by, and suddenly Jacob Isaac is home. It is night. In the bottom of the chest of drawers I find a nightgown that belonged to Feigaleh. I take off her dress, put on the nightdress, and approach Jacob Isaac, sitting on the chair, his head in his hands, and I gently caress his cheek as Feigaleh taught me to do. My thumb almost touches his lips. He freezes, and I slowly pull him to me.

"Come to me, my dear Jacob Isaac. Love and embrace me, and let us be one flesh." I see the shock on his face, but I am not put off. I take off the nightgown and stand before him, naked as the day I was born. In the morning, my head aches, and I feel pressure on my temples.

I don't know what happened during the night, and I want to throw up. I peek at Jacob Isaac's face and cannot read his expression.

"I feel strange," I say. "Perhaps I am ill."

"You are not well," he replies. "I will go to my friend Simcha Bunim. After all, he is a pharmacist, and perhaps he can help."

A SPIRIT THAT IS NOT A DYBBUK[14]

Sheindel continues her story:

"I learned what happened between Jacob Isaac and his friend, the pharmacist, only after my death, when I got here, to the world where it is possible to know everything.

"When Jacob Isaac entered Simcha Bunim's home, he didn't know how to start the conversation. Simcha welcomed his friend and began:

"If I were offered the choice of being as great as our forefather Abraham and he being like me – I would never agree." Simcha expected The Jew to be surprised at his remark because why wouldn't he agree to be great like our forefather, Abraham? But he saw that his friend did not react and went on to explain, without being asked to do so.

"What would the Creator have to gain if Abraham were Bunim and I were Abraham? Nothing good ever came out of substituting or from substitutes." Simcha observed the deepening vertical crease between Jacob Isaac's forehead and nose and asked what was troubling him.

"I don't know, my friend. Lately, Sheindel has been behaving strangely. She tries to seduce me, wearing Feigaleh's clothes and behaving as if she were her sister. She says weird

---

14. The possession of a living body by the soul of a deceased person.

78

things that don't seem to be coming from her. And she suddenly wakes up, feeling something is wrong with her, but she doesn't remember or know what happened to her. Is it possible that her sister's spirit can possess her?"

"As you know, I am not the person to ask that kind of question," said Simcha Bunim. "I don't believe in ghosts and spirits that dominate living people. I have other theories. But if we are prepared to listen to the stories of the healers around us, the Masters of the Good Name, it seems that in most cases the spirits that take over living people are men. Do you claim that the dybbuk that has taken hold of Sheindel is the spirit of her sister?"

"Yes, it's possible that a spirit entered her. You speak the truth when you say that most of the occupying spirits are men, and most of them enter young women like Sheindel… If we speak of Feigaleh's spirit, why did she choose Sheindel? What does she want of her?"

"You know that the spirit is seeking rectification in most cases."

"It doesn't make sense that Feigaleh would speak through Sheindel. Feigaleh was a good woman; if she had a problem that required a solution, I would certainly have felt it. And anyway, sinful souls usually enter others as dybbuks…"

"What happened? What made you think a dybbuk was involved?" Simcha Bunim inquired.

"It was weird. There was no rolling of eyes or a scary voice. Sheindel spoke with her own voice but out of semi-consciousness. We were in our room. I had almost fallen asleep. Suddenly I heard groans and heavy breathing. I thought Sheindel was having a dream, and I mumbled, "Shush… Shush… everything is all right…" She didn't respond or move. And the groans did not stop. I turned to her and embraced her, and suddenly, she pushed me roughly and aggressively said, "Don't touch her!"

"Who? Who mustn't I touch?" I asked. "Are you dreaming?" but she went wild and screamed, even though her eyes were still closed. "Betrayal, robbery, burglary, and treason," she said with the same intensity.

"What's happened, Sheindel? Wake up. Everything is all right," I said.

"I'm Feigaleh!" she said. "I'm Feigaleh! How could you forget me? There was a time when you couldn't live without me."

Jacob Isaac grew silent, and Simcha stared at him intently.

"When was the last time you thought about her?" he asked his friend.

"After her death, not an hour or a day passed without me thinking of her... I loved her, but lately, I am preoccupied with my disciples, with teaching..."

"Even after her death, there were followers. Nevertheless, there was not a day when you didn't mourn her passing."

"And I still bemoan my loss every hour of every day... And Sheindel senses this. In the early days of our marriage, I would sometimes forget myself on my way home, sure that I was about to meet her – Feigaleh, that is – and when I went into the warm house and was welcomed by the aroma of noodle soup, I would joyfully call out loud, 'Feigaleh, I'm here. I'm home!' And Sheindel, you know, was no more than a child then, and would run from the kitchen, panting and laughing."

"Feigaleh, is she here? Is Feigaleh here?"

"And I would say to her, 'Sheindel, it's a mistake. I was wrong. You know that Feigaleh is dead…'"

"Poor Sheindel," Simcha Bunim replied. "Your words must have hurt her. It's not easy to marry your sister's husband, especially after the great love you shared."

"Sheindel also loved her very much… but it was decreed that things would happen this way and not otherwise. If it weren't for Golda's prayer on our wedding day, and if she hadn't asked for a bridegroom like me for her younger daughter, everything could have been different."

"Yes, because you are unique and special, and no one else can compare with you… Don't look at me like that. I'm not being sarcastic. Were there more incidents when you mixed them up?"

"Sometimes, on a Sabbath eve when we make love, my thoughts chance to be with Feigaleh, but I immediately catch myself and mumble verses that remind me of the importance of the act and the purpose of the *mitzvah*,[15] and then I don't think of either of them."

"So do you still get confused between them sometimes?"

"No, I don't."

"So, what happened that night when Feigaleh spoke out of Sheindel's voice? Tell me exactly what happened and what was said. After all, it is known that if a spirit attaches itself to a person, especially a young woman, it is sometimes connected to matters between a man and a woman…"

"Are you saying that I didn't accurately regulate the course of the verses I was reciting?"

---

15. The Hebrew word *mitzvah* refers to a commandment commanded by God to be performed as a religious duty.

"I am not discussing you now. I'm talking about Sheindel. I'm talking about her needs and desires…" Jacob Isaac recalls words that Sheindel would whisper to him, "Let us be one flesh," and he replied, "It is said that a woman's desire is for her husband. There is nothing wrong with lust for a husband…"

And even the man himself is commanded to satisfy her desire…There is no evil in desiring your husband…The man, himself, is commanded to satisfy his wife's needs. And you will undoubtedly remember the words of The Preacher of Kozhnitz, who compared the love between Hashem and Israel to the love between the bridegroom and the bride who wed on Shavuot when the Torah was given…

"And suppose the bride finds favor in the eyes of the bridegroom, and the bridegroom in the eyes of the bride? In that case, they count the days to the time of their union and to becoming one, look forward to and long for the day of consummating their marriage… and at the right time the holiness comes from God through their being male and female; they are bridegroom and bride, and the more the bride decorates herself, the more she is the congregation of Israel. The bridegroom, as the Holy One, brings himself closer and closer to her… and a clever bride, even if she does not want the act of love, and has no desire to adorn herself and unite with her beloved, still shows a happy face until it appears to her husband that she is demanding it of him… But in truth, her intention is not for herself… If the bridegroom acknowledged this, he would do all in his power to add love for her…"

"Don't get side-tracked into idle sophistry, my dear Jacob Isaac," Simcha Bunim interrupted him gently. "You must concentrate on the main point, since we are talking about people's souls, about their lives…"

Jacob Isaac looked at Simcha's face in bewilderment and his eyebrows rose in amazement.

"We're not only talking about the spirit of Feigaleh, may she rest in peace," Simcha Bunim said to his friend. "And if indeed she seeks rectification, then it must be done because you know that lost souls always connect to the righteous. But I don't believe that we are dealing with a dybbuk. The spirits of women seeking rectification are women who have sinned, but both of us know that Feigaleh committed no sins, and if at night her desire arose, it is because that is the nature of a woman – as it is written, 'and your desire shall be for your husband…'

"A man of science am I, and I will tell you that no spirit or dybbuk speaks from Sheindel's mouth; only Sheindel herself speaks, and she believes that Feigaleh has taken possession of her because of her yearnings, because of her fears…"

Jacob Isaac stared at him in astonishment, and Simcha Bunim nodded and continued:

"We must not allow the situation to deteriorate…Sheindel must not forget herself in Feigaleh… You must take care of and, in particular, understand Sheindel, the young bride. How does she feel when you confuse her with her beloved sister? And if she has begun to love you after all these years that she was angry with you, after being forced to marry her adored sister's widower, and she cannot discuss her feelings with anyone… After all, she is far away from her home in Apt, from her parents, from the people she loves and is accustomed to… So now it is important to continue taking care of Sheindel. Perhaps you can send her to me, to my wife, and she will have someone to whom she can pour out her heart."

Sheindel continues telling her story. Tears well up in her eyes as she continues:

"When Jacob Isaac came home, we both pretended that nothing had happened. And again, at nightfall, I put on Feigaleh's nightdress, approached Jacob Isaac, and caressed his cheek with my thumb, almost touching his lips; once more, he froze, and I pulled him to me and said, "It's me, my beloved, your innocent wife. Come to me. Have mercy on me and come to my womb. Love me. And let your warmth spread through me and melt my coldness. And if God wills it, a child will be in my womb. Come to me softly, mercifully, or else, as you will see, my rage will burst out, and I will pour out my anger on you, break the boundaries of my soul, and leave it open to the cold outside. I plead for your mercy on my blood, spirit, and soul."

I remember how Jacob Isaac looked at me with tenderness and amazement and suddenly burst into song. It was the most beautiful sound I had heard in my entire life. I listened excitedly until my eyes closed and I fell asleep.

The next day – and that, too, was only revealed to me many years later – Jacob Isaac called on Simcha again and told him, "It was a good idea to bring my Sheindel closer to your wise woman, Rivka. I don't doubt that you were right. I heard Sheindel speaking yesterday, and it was not her voice or Feigaleh's, but a third voice. Indeed, she believes that Feigaleh's spirit has entered hers. More extreme measures than conversations with a clever woman are required. Some exorcism is necessary, even if we face an imagined dybbuk rather than a real one."

Simcha understood what troubled the heart of his good friend… and the pair began preparing what they would do to Sheindel – meaning to me, as I speak to you myself and tell you my story – an exorcism ceremony that isn't an expulsion. A mock expulsion ceremony. And precisely at this time, The Preacher of Kozhnitz was on his way to officiate at the marriage of the daughter of Shmuel Dov and Temer'l Bergson in Warsaw and passed through Peshischa on the way. When he arrived, the two of them, The Jew and his friend Simcha Bunim, asked him to carry out the expulsion ceremony. Heavy rain was falling then, and the whole yard was filled with sticky mud. Jacob Isaac instructed me to stay in my room on the morning of the ceremony. He spoke firmly, so I obeyed him, stayed in my room, and didn't even enter the adjacent room where he sat and studied. I heard the sounds of perplexing preparations coming from the room.

After a while, through the window, I saw Jacob Isaac laying planks on the muddy earth at the entrance to the house. From what I could see, a wagon stopped at the entrance, and a man of short stature was getting off. I understood why the planks were needed. He was aided by Jacob Isaac and Simcha Bunim, who both continued to support him, one on his right side and the other on his left, as he walked on the planks leading from the wagon to the house. I understood that he was an important person from the manner of his reception. The Preacher was a tiny man, delicate and soft. He was so slight that, but for the furs that covered his body, he would have been carried off in the wind like a dry leaf, and I thought how good it was that Jacob Isaac and Simcha Bunim were holding on to him, lest he take off and disappear. Sounds of dragging arose from the adjacent room, and when the door to my room suddenly opened, and I was invited to join the men, I was very puzzled to see that the red drape that always covered the Holy Ark was replaced by a black one. Seven black candles had been lit on the table; two men stood there together with Jacob Isaac, and the three were draped in their prayer shawls.

Jacob Isaac presented them to me.

"This is Rabbi Israel, known as The Preacher of Kozhnitz," he said. And I immediately drowned in the gentle gray eyes of that small, scrawny man. I felt like one sometimes feels on meeting someone for the first time – someone who was a stranger until that moment, although at first glance you feel as though you have come home, that he is a loving member of your family, that your soul is familiar to his.

"And you know Simcha Bunim, the pharmacist? Perhaps you remember him from the pharmacy...?"

I didn't remember him because the only time I went to the pharmacy there was a woman who introduced herself as Rivka.

"No, we've never met," the pharmacist said. "Perhaps you met Rivka, my wife. She's a clever woman who advises me, helps me in all matters, and also in the pharmacy."

I liked him immediately because that's how a man should relate to his wife.

"And they have come here specially to help you."

I looked into Rabbi Israel's eyes and almost dived into them because they had so much love. But as soon as the ceremony began, his whole appearance changed. He spoke to me aggressively and raised his voice.

"Look at me. Don't turn away. Look at me!" he ordered.

Once again, his eyes did not express that same tenderness and closeness, and I looked away from him.

"I order you to look up and see my face."

And when I looked at him, he asked, "Who are you?"

"I am Sheindel," I replied.

"I'm not talking to Sheindel. Who are *you*? Who has joined Sheindel? Your presence here is forbidden! You must leave at once!"

I began to scream and cry and realized I could no longer hide what had happened over the last few nights, so I screamed, "I'm Feigaleh! I'm Feigaleh! I won't go! This is where I belong and where I'll stay!"

"What did you come for here? Why do you want to stay? After all, you don't belong here."

"This is where I belong, and this is my home! I am Jacob Isaac's bride. And this is his house."

"You are forbidden to be here. Who permitted you to enter Sheindel?"

"Sheindel herself asked me! She called me to come."

"I forbid you to remain in Sheindel under any circumstances! I command you to leave her without mutilating any part of her body, not a tendon or an organ. Sheindel is now Jacob Isaac's wife. She is his bride. And you must go in peace to your fate…."

After I calmed down and stopped shaking, The Preacher looked at me warmly again and placated me with kind words.

"Have no fear, Sheindel," he said. "This is how it was meant to be. But from now on, you will know only good things. I will give you a talisman and write only blessings for your well-being in them. Until now, life has been difficult for you, but you will recover, be with child and bear a son, and his name will be Asher, after Jacob Isaac's father."

And Simcha Bunim also added his good wishes, too.

"We know that you miss your mother, Golda, in Apt. And from today, Rivka, my wife, will visit you."

The last to speak was Jacob Isaac, who said, "I know you miss Feigaleh, but you are my wife now, Sheindel. You are my wife."

And I did not know it immediately, but with the passing of days, I understood how good the ceremony had been. How clever and merciful the three men – Jacob Isaac, Simcha Bunim, and The Preacher of Kozhnitz – were. How wise and compassionate of them to know it was not about a real dybbuk, and how astute and merciful they were to understand that Feigaleh had not sinned, and neither had I. And how intelligent and forgiving of them to hide the ceremony and carry it out in our house rather than in a synagogue in the presence of ten men, of a minyan, as customarily accepted, so that the matter would remain discreet and unknown to the public. It would also not be remembered or written in any book that a dybbuk and my sister's spirit had taken control of my body and would only be recalled in your book, in the way it happened, ensconced in love and good intentions.

After these events, life gradually found pleasant avenues of routine. Rivka and I visited one another frequently, and with Rivka's help, I grew acquainted with and learned the ways of the world I lived in, the world of Hassids and righteous men. Simcha Bunim was already a follower of The Seer of Lublin, and even though he, like many others, tried to convince The Jew to study with The Seer, my Jacob Isaac refused to do that.

"I don't want," he repeatedly said, "to bask in the shadow of a righteous man."

All of this was told to me by Rivka. She also explained that many people spoke highly of Jacob Isaac, The Seer of Lublin. She spoke of his great powers to influence the supernal world and our own world, and his ability to bring down the Divine abundance for the benefit of his followers and all who turned to him for help.

WARP AND WOOF

Four Jewish Brides.

The four of them are dressed in white. Four beautiful young, happy brides. Four smiling, laughing brides. A soft light illuminates them.

Two of them stand, the third is seated, and the fourth leans over her. They are preoccupied with themselves and unaware of what is happening around them. Their white clothes are no more than shrouds. White shrouds, some of them have crumbled. The four form a circle and start dancing, and their movements resemble floating. Miriam and Sheindel enter the circle, and Sheindel turns to me and says, "I, Sheindel, will tell the story of Miriam and the story of her righteous man, The Seer."

And so Sheindel says…

Miriam disappeared. No one knew where she was. They searched for her, of course, but not as they would search for someone they wanted to find. They went here and there, paused for a while on the banks of the river because the event took place in the late winter when the days were a little warmer and the ice on the river had begun to crack. But not a trace of her was found. She had been shut up in her house for three years. It was better that the neighbors didn't see her so they wouldn't remember the story of how her bridegroom left her on the eve of their marriage while she was dancing, and the sad misfortune that had befallen her.

Only her grandfather wept from the bottom of his heart and blamed himself, for he had arranged the match with the brilliant student with extraordinary qualities, one of which had given him the name of . . . "The Seer."

Already as a child, Jacob Isaac Horowitz, known as The Seer, knew how to discern what kind of seed people came from by looking at their facial features – whether they were from the seed of Cain or the seed of Abel, whether they were sinners or righteous, or whether they were destined to harm or to help; from their facial features he was able to observe the inner structure of their souls, to know how many incarnations they have had behind them, and how many still await them. Since it had been difficult for him as a child, he decided to cover his eyes and not look at people. He would constantly look down so that he saw nothing but the place on which his feet stepped. How could he live for seven years without looking at the trees blossoming, the water flowing in the river, the ripples on its surface, and the flowers in the spring?

How can you live seven whole years and notice the change of seasons only by how your feet walk – whether the road is muddy or scorched? And what happens to your soul if, for seven whole years, you don't see the faces and expressions of people, whether distant or close?

He probably removed the blindfold when he was alone, locked in his room, and perhaps looked out of his window at the view that unfolded in the sky through it, changing its colors throughout the passing of the days and seasons. Maybe that window was his only connection to the visible world, and so it was precisely through one that he chose to jump to his death, knowing that we would use this inappropriate phrase to describe what happened. But let's not get ahead of what comes later.

In time, they matched him with the beautiful maiden, a young daughter of a good family from a small village near Krasnobród. Her grandfather was proud of the match. He loved his granddaughter deeply. Already as an infant, she would stare into his eyes and flash smiles that brightened his day. He didn't know what made him happier – the two dimples in her cheeks or the two little white teeth that peeped out of her mouth – and he promised himself that when the time came for her to get married, he would choose the most brilliant, holiest scholar because that was the custom in our time. Exceptionally brilliant Yeshiva students were matched with wealthy families. No, I am not confused when I say the bridegrooms were matched to the wealthy, since they rarely asked the brides' opinions. This was how the honorable grandfather found a suitable bridegroom for his beloved granddaughter: the successful Jacob Isaac Horowitz, Rabbi Elimelech's student, whose great gift of vision was well known.

It came to pass on the day before the marriage ceremony, at the time of the traditional bridegroom's feast, when the bridegroom asked to see his bride's face. The bridegroom refused to enter the inner room, in which the embarrassed bride awaited her bridegroom and insisted that she be brought to him in the presence of all the diners. All those present were amazed that this young man, famous for his Torah learning and faith, was not ashamed and even demanded to see the young girl, except that the bridegroom reminded them of what is written in the marriage tractate that forbids a man to sanctify his bride until he sees her. And since he based his wish on the words of wise men, they brought the girl to him.[16]

The grandfather expected only good things to happen following the match. He was proud of his granddaughter and knew that she was flawless but for a small scar on her forehead. He was confident that a wise scholar would not attach importance to such a small matter. Nevertheless, he was concerned. He told himself that his identification with his granddaughter was the source of his concern. Obviously, it is an embarrassing task for a young girl like his grand-daughter to enter a room clouded in pipe smoke and bustling with men, to be precise, and to know that she is being examined like an animal. A terrible thought also flashed through his mind concerning the arrogance of this bride-groom, who asks to see the girl in the middle of a reception, and wonders whether his granddaughter felt like Vashti in her time when she was called to the reception of King Ahasuerus, who wanted to show off and boast about her beauty. He hurriedly rejected such a thought because although Ahasuerus was arrogant and stupid, Vashti herself was not worthy of words of praise. At the same time, as he knew, his granddaughter was a young woman full of virtue and willing to please. And because this was her nature, and she was unlike Vashti, she did not refuse the invitation. She entered the room and glanced into the eyes of the intended bridegroom.

When Jacob Isaac Horowitz saw his intended bride, he blanched, and she knew that something awful had

---

16. Massekhet Ketubot: Introduction to the Tractate.

happened but didn't know what. Those present also felt that something had gone wrong, but did not know what it was until the bridegroom opened his mouth and said that he wanted to cancel the wedding because he did not see the image of God in her face – rather he saw two lines like warp and weft – one horizontal and the other perpendicular. He saw the image of the cross on the beautiful, golden-haired, blue-eyed girl's face. And because he saw the picture of the cross, he insisted on immediately canceling the marriage and would not even wait until the end of the feast.

A commotion broke out. Even the groom's father didn't know what to say, although one thing was sure: The girl and her family must not be harmed now in public; fearing what people would say convinced the son not to cancel the wedding.

"If you do not wish to consummate the marriage, you are not obliged to," his father told him, "and if you insist, you can give her a divorce immediately. But you cannot get out of marrying her."

The young groom relented, promised his father he would go through with the marriage ceremony, and swore an oath to honor him.

Immediately after the ceremony and before the marriage's consummation, the bride's father was still dancing the wedding dance with her as she held the bridegroom's father's girdle on one side and her father held it on the other. Her eyes lit up. The young bridegroom, Jacob Isaac, entered the room where the bride and groom would be alone for the first time immediately after the ceremony. After he handed the divorce decree to a trusted messenger, he escaped through the window, wearing only his bridegroom's clothes, and made his getaway from there, never to return.

It was cold outside. Snow began to fall. He had no money in his pocket and was trying to go to his rabbi on foot, to Rabbi Elimelech from the city of Lizhensk. The Seer was a mere boy and, in his lightweight shoes and white silk coat he was barely visible in the snow falling around and covering the earth. If a carriage had passed along the way, the coachman probably would not have seen him. The severe cold penetrated his thin wedding clothes, the wind began to blow, and a fierce storm raged. And the young Jacob Isaac ran so he would not freeze, God forbid. His hurried escape landed him in a forest, where he suddenly came upon a wooden hut; when he opened the door, he felt a pleasant warmth in the house. He sat on one of the armchairs and saw images of people around him dressed in black, welcoming him cheerfully and congratulating him on getting to the hostel and saving his life from the horrors of the storm outside. Then the innkeeper – a tall, slim, beautiful woman dressed in black lace – came in and called the visitors to dinner. Jacob Isaac hesitated, not knowing if the visitors were of his faith or if the food was kosher, but then the beautiful woman turned to him and asked him to remain in the reception room and dine with her. Wearing splendid uniforms, the waiters entered carrying a silver platter of steaming stuffed chickens and clear soup with dumplings in a tureen decorated with drawings of blue fowls with gilded cockscombs. They lay the feast on a small table beside the crimson velvet sofa. The innkeeper turned to the young Jacob Isaac and invited him to sit beside her on the couch, telling him that she is a free woman, available for love, and that she desires him. She reminds Jacob Isaac about

Potiphar's wife's attempt to seduce Joseph in Egypt, and understanding that he is in great danger, he tells the beautiful woman, in whose face he saw there was neither the woof and the warp nor the image of a cross – that he had sworn an oath to do everything to bring satisfaction to the Holy One, Blessed be He, and asked her what joy would be caused to God if he were to consent to her temptation. Instead of getting an answer, he found himself in the dark forest, where the treetops hid the sky and the moon, leaving only darkness and freezing cold. When dawn came, he saw a faraway inn resembling a regular hostel. He asked the Hassid named Daniel, who managed it, to help him get to Rabbi Elimelech of Lizhensk. Daniel the Hassid gave Jacob Isaac regular warm clothing, food, and drink, and ordered a carriage to take him to his destination. When Jacob Isaac reached his home, Rabbi Elimelech greeted him with the following words:

"Welcome, Joseph the Righteous; the villain has lost his game!

By "the villain," he was referring to Samael, who had tried to entrap the soul of the righteous youth.

Thus the story of his unfortunate marriage is told in a way that is meant to enhance and praise the image of a virtuous young man who was miraculously saved by the gift of his vision from marrying a girl with the woof and warp on her face, and from a temptress innkeeper, who also tried to seduce many others. Many good people wrote about her, since the image of the temptress innkeeper fired the imagination of the foremost writers, but abandoned Miriam – that's what we'll call her – on the dance floor, grasping the splendid girdle. No one wonders what became of her.

What did she feel? What could that girl, abandoned by the man who would in time, become known by his followers as "The Angel" expect after she was abandoned by the perfect young man gifted with extraordinary vision? Wouldn't they be wise to distance themselves from her? After all, who knows what he saw on her face when he escaped on that thunderous, stormy night? And for as long as she stays in her parents' house, no one will ever want to marry her sisters and brothers, as she is evidence of an awful, terrifying, primeval sin that has affected her and all her family, a sin of unknown dimension but well enough recognized to frighten the man of vision away from her. She is dependent on her parents and cannot provide for herself. Even if she were to seek employment as a governess of children, no one would employ her because no family would want such a governess to educate its children. The young holy man left her in the lurch, leaving her no choice but to seek her fate far away from there.

Later it was told that he had discovered in her evil spirits from the world of impurity that had tried to entrap him and prevent him from reaching the world of holiness. After that, people also said she had turned to sinful ways; she had probably converted to Christianity, and they added as proof the cross her bridegroom had seen on her forehead. To where she had disappeared? No one knew.

Maybe she had turned to the Turkowice monastery, close to the city of Lublin. Perhaps she did walk off to the monastery one day, asked for refuge, and cared for orphaned children there and, with the love she showered on them, managed to drown her yearnings for a family of her own. Perhaps she worked in the monastery's vegetable garden

97

and grew accustomed to keeping her silence. A high wall enclosed the monastery; no one could have seen those who found refuge there. Perhaps she chose that monastery without knowing that her intended bridegroom would move to Lublin one day. It is quite possible that one day the rumor reached her of the wonders performed for the Jews by Rabbi Jacob Isaac, who lived in Lublin. Maybe the gentiles who were part of the auxiliary help at the monastery talked about him. Or perhaps she was filled with thoughts of the man who had deserted her and was living well. But all these thoughts are in the realm of misleading and doubtful surmise as to whether or not certain rumors were facts because no one had ever really searched for Miriam after her disappearance. And since she had accustomed herself to silence and apparently had not shared the events of her story with anyone, she also spoke little with any of us. We don't know whether she changed her name from Miriam to Maria or chose a completely different name that would not recall her past each time anyone approached to ask who she was and what became of her.

THE OTHER JACOB ISAAC
SON OF MATIL

And Sheindel continues her story:

After he divorced Miriam, "The Seer" joined the court of Rabbi Elimelech. Not many days later, after appearing at the court, they were already in a rush to have him marry Tehila Shprintze, the daughter of an established family. Tehila was a good woman from a reputable family, compassionate and merciful, although not a great beauty, and did not uplift his soul, yet The Seer was happy with her because she bore no unique signs – not on her face and, more importantly, not on her forehead. Moreover, all those who met her and looked at her couldn't recall her facial features, which had faded in their memory and at the moment they beheld her. Her body was angular, and her clothes never made her shapely. She was quiet, not talkative, and her eyes were always lowered, looking at the floor, like The Seer in his youth. What the rabbi read on her forehead, he never told. He probably saw nothing; perhaps he only saw that she was shy and humble or interpreted her modesty as a positive quality, but this may be doubtful – with no offense to the truth. He probably saw her always staying in his shadow and found that to be a positive trait. Had she directed her gaze at him, he would have noticed that her eyes were gray, and their beauty was worthy of praise. But since she constantly lowered her eyes and didn't look into the eyes of people facing her, her long eyelashes couldn't be revealed in all their beauty and could only cast a shadow on her face and blur her image even more. And when she went out to the marketplace, she was treated like a simple woman, and no one recognized her as the great Rebbetzin of Lublin, the wife of the righteous man. With the passing years, she preferred to remain cloistered in her home, where she walked around like a shadow. But she had a great soul, and The Seer recognized this. It is told that one Sabbath, there was no money in the house for groceries, so she stood on the street corner, begging for money. A rough-looking passer-by threw her two small coins. She thanked him and blessed him, "May you be blessed. May the light of the Sabbath guide you on your way."

On that day, during the evening prayer, the soul of The Seer rose to the heavens, and there he witnessed a debate between the heavenly angels, who called on Jacob Isaac to settle the dispute because on the one hand, the Rebbetzin blessed someone with the light of the Sabbath, but on the other, the man who received the blessing was a crude soul, unworthy of such a valuable Sabbath blessing. The Seer of Lublin pondered the matter and determined that "The man who was blessed is indeed uncouth and unworthy of such supernal light," the Seer of Lublin agreed. "But isn't it possible that he is so coarse because he doesn't have the light of the Sabbath? If he receives the light of Sabbath, he will cease to be crude and worthless."

In time, The Seer succeeded in controlling his frightening power to stare at people's foreheads and determine the former incarnations of their souls. Everyone knew that if The

Seer were to glance at their foreheads, not only would their souls immediately be revealed to him, but also their incarnations from the distant past, until he would know whether they descended from Cain the sinner or Abel the innocent.

He was terrified on the days when he saw the mysteries of souls, even when he didn't want to, because he saw not only the attributes of awe of the soul but also its relations with the "Other Side" – with Satan, may God protect us. As we have already been told, in his youth he would cover his eyes with a white cloth to not see the faces of the "other" and the horrors of the consuming fire. His eyes were covered with a white cloth for almost his entire youth. He didn't look at anything, and only listened to the words of Rabbi Elimelech in the Beit Midrash. Only at night did he remove the white cloth from his eyes to study the letters of the sacred texts and memorize the issues studied that day. But in time, when he matured, he learned how to balance between the souls, to soften the terrifying sight with the image of the souls huddling beside the angels at the foot of the throne of honor, and he also learned how not to stare at peoples' foreheads. He got used to focusing his gaze on the face of the person in front of him, between his mouth and nose. In this way, he would learn the proportions of the face and only then turn his gaze slightly and carefully upward until he looked into the eyes of the person standing before him. Still, he climbed only up to the eyes and not higher than that to the forehead because then, as he knew, the screen over the person's soul would be lifted, and all the history of his soul would be revealed to him.

He was the first and foremost of Rabbi Elimelech's students and, with the passing of the years, felt that he had nothing more to learn from his teacher, so he decided to move with some of his followers to the city of Łańcut. There, he set up a study group close to the palace of Count Potocki. Still, when The Seer learned how much his move hurt Rabbi Elimelech when he understood that his followers were stopping at Łańcut, and were not continuing on to Lizhensk, The Seer decided to move to the great city of Lublin, where he set up his famous Beit Midrash on Shiroka Street, close to the Palace. Thousands flocked to his court to hear Torah, and he taught them to act humbly, to love others, and to be virtuous.

But then came a time when The Seer felt that his best days had passed because it had been some time since he last received any special enlightenment. He had already stopped counting the days, which added up to weeks, and then years, during which he had not opened the books of memories in which he would write down all the sublime and latent things that were revealed to him at the time when he detached himself from his corporeality and wandered around in the supernal worlds. Indeed, he still visited those worlds, but no new secrets were revealed, and he knew that the significance of this was that he had ceased to ascend the stairs.

Not only did he stop coming up with innovations to renew Torah, he also felt that he was deficient in his role as a wise man who influences his followers by bringing down material welfare of the Divine abundance from the supernal world to their own world. His followers made pilgrimages to him to seek his closeness and find the light, but felt that the joy of life had left him, and he confessed this to his close friends, "They ask for enlightenment from me, but I don't have light. I am in the dark."

And he already asked for his heir to come to him and replace him. What were the thoughts of the Rabbi of Lublin
when he prayed to God to show him who would succeed
him? It was hard to know. Did he want to see because he
feared that an heir would grab hold of his position while he
was still alive, just as he had done to his own rabbi, Rabbi
Elimelech? It was reasonable to assume that he wanted to
know who he was so that he could inaugurate his successor
in his own way. At any rate, he prayed to God to show him
in his lifetime who would replace him after his death, and
the heavens replied that the name of his heir would be Jacob Isaac, the son of Matil. The Seer was also called Jacob
Isaac, and his mother is also Matil. And in his heart, he said
it was good. Here is the man who will take my place and be
exactly like me; they won't notice the difference.

So when a young scholar named Jacob Isaac, son of
Matil, arrived at his court, he welcomed him warmly. On
the night of Shabbat, as was his custom, The Seer held a
feast for his followers and seated Jacob Isaac in the place of
honor beside him. But when the guest was invited to deliver a Biblical discourse, he refused and said he preferred to
listen and learn. His remarks pleased The Seer, who pre-
sumed that the younger Jacob Isaac was modest and humble. But after a while, the image of the same Jacob Isaac, son
of Matil, began to trouble his peace of mind, and a cloud of
puzzlement shaded The Seer's thoughts.

Although The Seer had asked not to review the past
souls of the students around him because he felt that
seeing all their deeds over all the generations damaged his
ability to love them and encourage them to be merciful,
the behavior of Jacob Isaac caused him to deviate from

his custom. This was because it became clear that despite their identical names, Jacob Isaac was completely different from The Seer. Nothing about Jacob Isaac, son of Matil, the student, resembled Jacob Isaac, son of Matil, the teacher. Although he had already managed to change the young man's doctrine and explained to him that the role of the righteous person is to be meek and humble, to distance himself from prestige, and acknowledge his inferiority so that he can reach the expansion of the soul and removal of the physical corporeality, he must also be a lover of people to be able to bring down the abundance and the good of the supernal worlds to the community and his followers. He found before him a man with strange customs that proved to him that he was not meek and modest or loved people as required. Therefore, he did not hold back and looked at his forehead and found that he was two-faced, that his inner spirit was not as he appeared. He said one thing and meant another. His negative opinion of his student was bolstered when other students complained that Jacob Isaac, son of the other Matil, was arrogant and proud.

The Seer turned to Rabbi David of Lelov, his follower, and discussed the problem with him.

Jacob Isaac held Rabbi David in high regard because he knew he was full of love for every man and every living creature. I have already told you that when Rabbi David would come to the tavern in Apt, he would arrive with water and fodder for the horses. And when he would travel with other Hassidim to Lublin, hire a wagon with them, and see another Hassid on the way, they would give him a ride and continue like that until the load became too heavy for the horses. Oh – then they'd all disembark, leaving only the cargo on board, and they would walk behind the wagon to avoid overburdening the horses. So The Seer knew what a good man Rabbi David was and how good his deeds were, and he also knew that he had the power to do good, because in return for his good deed of feeding the horses and his acts of mercy, on Rosh Hashana the heavens opened up. The Seer approached Rabbi David of Lelov and asked him if he had the good fortune to meet students worthy of greatness on his travels in Poland. Rabbi David told him about Jacob Isaac from Peshischa.

"And Jacob Isaac – is he a Hassid?" The Seer asked Rabbi David.

"No," replied Rabbi David, "but he is a brilliant student."

"Why isn't he a Hassid? Is he an opponent of Hassidism?"assidHass

Rabbi David chuckled and answered, "Please forgive me, Rabbi. I wasn't laughing out of contempt. But Jacob Isaac is very far from the politics and power struggles between the supporters of Hassidism and those who oppose it! The only thing that interests him is studying Torah."

"And do you know his parents?"

Rabbi David spoke enthusiastically of his father, Rabbi Asher, and he added and revealed that the uncle of Jacob Isaac of Peshischa was one of the thirty-six Hidden Righteous Men.[17]

"And what is his mother's name?" asked The Seer.

---

17. According to tradition, every generation has thirty-six great righteous people who can perform wondrous acts, but the generation is not deserving of them, so the stature of these righteous people is hidden, except to a few, and they are not known to the public; sometimes they are wood-choppers or water-drawers.

"She is a woman of valor. And if I'm not mistaken, I believe her name is Matil." The Seer grew very excited, and he turned to Rabbi David and said, "I have a request to make of you, and it is imperative that you bring this Jacob Isaac, the son of Asher and Matil, to me!"

So when Rabbi David came to Peshischa, he saw Jacob Isaac and his friend Yeshayah sitting engrossed in their studies. Rabbi David entered and listened to what they were saying. He wanted to avoid disturbing them and waited until one of them rose to go to the bookshelf to take out a volume. Rabbi David took advantage of the break and said to them, "The Talmudic verse isn't as important as the action," and he left the room. The two could not ignore Rabbi David's comment.

"That is so true," Jacob Isaac said to Yeshaya. "People talk and make declarations, but they don't take responsibility for their fate or practice the things they preach. Where did Rabbi David acquire such wisdom?"

They closed their Talmudic texts, ran after Rabbi David, and asked him where he learned such wisdom.

"In Lublin," he said, "from the Rabbi of Lublin. Go there."

When they entered the room of The Seer, the latter gazed at the forehead of our Jacob Isaac and was filled with joy at finding intelligence and modesty there as well as everything necessary for the one who was worthy of inheriting his place as the shepherd of the flock.

The Jew was almost 30 years old when he first arrived in Lublin. He had already reached great heights, and The Seer, aware of his spiritual stature and the importance he attached to studying and thought, asked him to assist him and teach his most brilliant students. It was not fitting to call the rabbi and his pupil by the same name, and that was why the students called Jacob Isaac, the son of Matil from Peshischa, "The Jew from Peshischa." They called him by that name because every time he came up with a critical Torah innovation, he modestly said, "That original thought is not mine. I heard it from a 'Jew' that I met."

From then on, My Jew would travel again and again to his rabbi in Lublin, return, and immediately travel back again. Like my sister, I also learned the taste of loneliness because the road to the city of Lublin is long. The Hassids would remain there for an extended time once they reached it, out of their desire to study and learn the way of their rabbi in Hassidism. And I know that many were amazed that The Jew actually chose The Seer to be his rabbi. It was acknowledged by all connected to the facts that The Jew's wisdom was superior to that of his rabbi, The Seer – the Rabbi of Lublin. It is also known that the Rabbi of Lublin, Rabbi Azriel Horowitz, who was called "Ironhead" because of his great wisdom, was one of the principal opponents of The Seer and was especially critical, not only because he didn't esteem, but rather opposed Hassidism, but also because he did not respect The Seer as an astute scholar. Once the Ironhead asked The Seer himself why dozens of students come to him despite his not being a great Torah scholar.

"That I don't know," The Seer answered him. Ironhead said, "Next Shabbat, confess to your pupils that you are not great in Torah." So that's exactly what The Seer did – and look at what a wonder took place the following week: Even more followers came to the rabbi! Ironhead told him, "They probably came because they thought you were a man of great reserve and modesty. Tell them this coming Sabbath that you are a learned man; that way they will understand that you are neither meek nor modest, and they will not turn up."

The Seer replied, "But I cannot do that! I cannot tell a lie."

Ironhead went to The Jew himself and asked him, "Why do you, the learned genius, consider The Seer to be your rabbi? Even he knows his mediocrity and transfers his brilliant pupils to you."

The Jew responded that he learns about life from The Seer.

"I learned every detail of my life from him, even how to sleep. The Seer taught me how to fall asleep as soon as I lie down."

But The Jew did not want to be a replacement for The Seer. He listened to the theory of the righteous from his rabbi but refused to accept it for himself, and in principle refused to adopt the part that relates to the role of the righteous in this world. He disagreed with The Seer's concept, according to which the righteous are supposed to bring down abundance from the supernal world and give it to their followers, affecting their well-being on the material level. The Seer believed that after all, from well-being they will recognize the greatness of God and adhere to spirituality.

In his view, the Hassids were exempt from any spiritual effort on their own behalf, and the one who must strive for them is their righteous leader. The Jew, on the other hand, preferred to place the responsibility on the followers themselves – both the responsibility for their material condition and, not least, for their spiritual condition.

On the days when The Jew stayed at his home in

Peshischa, many of The Seer's followers who did not want to stop studying would come to him; this provoked the anger of The Seer. He was convinced that The Jew was building his own court, which hurt him. He forgot how he established a court at Lancut while Rabbi Elimelech was still alive and went as far as Lublin because what he had done had turned the rabbi's disciples against him. If he had given the matter some thought, he would have understood that this was the way of the world. However, he was furious with The Jew and would send people to Peshischa to spy on him and check whether he called himself "Rebbe" in front of his students.

And what else did they say about The Seer? They say that more than anything, he was strict about "protecting his eyes" from looking at women, and even demanded the same of his students. And it is also told that he once traveled to visit the person who was his rabbi, Rabbi Shmelke from Nikolsburg, a city that was more modern than Lublin in its way of life. The Seer tied a kerchief over his eyes so he wouldn't see the women. A woman noticed this and burst out laughing. The rabbi was angry with her and bore a grudge because of it. At any rate, the woman fell ill. When this became known to Rabbi Shmelke, he told The Seer, "Go away, and don't come back. You have no business in our town."

He once visited Rabbi Boruch of Medzhybizh, who would deliver the sermon at the third Shabbat meal. It was customary in Medzhybizh that all the followers would sit around the Shabbat table and listen to the rabbi's sermon, while the women and girls would listen to him as they stood in the entrance to the room. The Seer was astonished that they allowed the women to enter the room and listen to Torah over the heads of the men, and he complained to Rabbi Boruch, "After all, it is written: Let my eyes not see deceptive visions. And how do you allow this?"

Rabbi Boruch answered, "Even if there was all the vanity in the world here, my eyes would not see it."

And, I tell you that despite all his attempts, The Seer actually did look and see.

ILLUMINATING BLUE EYES

Four Jewish Brides.

The four of them are dressed in white. Four beautiful, young, happy brides. Four smiling, laughing brides. A soft light illuminates them.

Two of them stand, the third is seated, and the fourth leans over her. They are preoccupied with themselves and unaware of what is happening around them. Their white clothes are no more than shrouds. White shrouds, some of which have crumbled. The four form a circle and start dancing, and their movements resemble floating. Beilah and Sheindel enter the circle, and Sheindel turns to me and says, "I, Sheindel, will tell the story of Beilah."

And so Sheindel tells the story.

Beilah was beautiful and wild. She had coal-black hair and eyes of a deep shade of blue that one was drawn to stare at more and more to identify the exact shade of blue or purple that a brief glance could not satisfy. When I saw her for the first time, I felt a long wrinkle forming a longitudinal line down the center of my forehead as I struggled to understand and define the color of her eyes. She had spirit and seemed unable to stand in one place without moving. She was frenetic. And if you want to grasp how beautiful she was, look at Elizabeth Taylor in the movie of Shakespeare's

"The Taming of the Shrew." Like her, Beilah was wild and sensuous. Although indeed, her breasts and hair were always covered – her breasts, always, and her hair, from the day she was married – but even though her hair was firmly tied, it was impossible to ignore the pulsating and tremors that burned in her, which she cooled with long sprints from place to place. She never took dainty steps but always raced, her eyes fiery and her cheeks blazing. And you will recall that we are describing events that occurred a long time ago – more than two-hundred years, no? And after all, it wasn't acceptable in those times for a woman to run around in the streets like that, especially as she ties the edges of her dress around her legs so they won't trip her, and when she ran, her slim ankles were visible, although they were covered with thick stockings.

Despite her wildness and the fire contained within her, or perhaps because of it, the suitors who wanted to marry her fought over her.

Moreover, she was the daughter of a respected family of learned people. Every time her hand in marriage was sought, her brother would go to Lublin to ask The Seer what he thought of the match. The Seer always mulled the matter over seriously and then asked to examine the forehead of the intended bridegroom to discover the lineage of his soul. As soon as he looked at the prospective bridegroom, he covered his eyes with his hand and said, "No, she deserves a greater soul than his."

And when Beilah's brother went home and shook his head to convey the negative opinion, tears would well up in Beilah's violet-blue eyes. She would storm out of the house like a strong wind and run this way and that, and on returning home would drink cold water from the pitcher, get into bed and cover her face with the heavy coverlet. When the same thing happened repeatedly, Beilah shrugged as if she had lost hope. And the marriage proposals grew fewer and further apart. The matchmakers began avoiding her because the candidates she turned down had difficulty making a match after that. Who knows what The Seer saw at the root of their souls that made him disapprove of them as suitors for Beilah? Indeed, The Seer repeatedly explained that they had no faults to prevent them from marrying other women. It was because Beilah was intended for a great, pure soul that had not yet revealed itself. Nevertheless, people are suspicious by nature, and no one imagined that when The Seer remained a widower after Tehila Shprintze died, he would hurriedly request Beilah's hand and marry her.

This was not the husband Beilah had prayed for. She was several decades younger than he, and in her dreams she had hoped for a man like herself – strapping and powerful, perhaps even a little wild. When the two of them were led to the marriage canopy, it was impossible not to notice the difference between her blushing face and supple body and his pale face and careful, measured steps. He walked like someone who feared he might trip and fall.

Only then did it become clear that he had always wanted her, knew what the future would bring, and perhaps even kept her for himself. However, the desire that burned in him did not give her a child. In the first days after the wedding, Beilah was preoccupied with being The Seer's wife, a rebbetzin, and the rabbi's spouse. Life at the rabbi's court was interesting. Throngs of Hassidim came to hear his every word, and on the Sabbath he would host all those who presented themselves as his followers for meals, whether they were or not. Sometimes Jews came to Lublin in the course of doing business in the big city and trying to save on their expenses; they would come and enjoy the Sabbath hospitality of The Seer because they knew that if they said they were his followers, they would enjoy free meals.

It is told that once Rabbi David of Lelov came to his rabbi, The Seer, for the Sabbath and was held up on his way at one of the neighboring villages because in every village he came to he would spend many hours with the Jews who lived there. Rabbi David hadn't paid attention to the hour and knew he could not get to Lublin in time, so he stayed in that village. He regretted it so much that it occurred to him that if all those who wanted to spend the Sabbath with The Seer actually came, the table would have been so long that it would have reached as far as the village where he was at the time; he immediately felt the joy of the Sabbath and told the Hassids with him that they were actually dining at the rabbi's table. His thinking was not that far from the truth because usually the number of people at the Sabbath table of the rabbi was in the dozens, if not the hundreds.

At first, Beilah busied herself with the Shabbat shopping and the management of the cooking and baking, which demanded hours and hours of planning and organization. Still, it turned out that this work had been done in the same format for many years and was new only to her; she soon realized that the cooks and bakers knew very well what they had to prepare and did not need her to remind them.

Life at home was rather boring, and therefore she warmly received the guests visiting her home, aiming to be included in the internal politics of the court. She especially loved her conversations with Yekutiel, who shared information about The Jew's activities with her.

The Jew was a fine-looking, healthy man, who looked at her face – unlike the others, who lowered their gaze in her presence as if to say, "I know precisely who you are."

His gaze, and the feeling he aroused in her, made her angry with him, and she enjoyed hearing criticism of him.

People gossiped to her and told tales about The Jew attempting to unseat her husband and replace him as the leader of his Hassids. Beilah delighted in the Hassidic political machinations, but that was spoiled by the fact that The Seer himself did not cooperate with her. Each time she complained to him about The Jew, he would shrug it off dismissively as if to say "Why should I deal with insignificant matters when there are more important things to do?" And she thought he was referring to the child that she had not borne him. The Jew, on his part, also heard the rumors and gossip and knew that she was undermining him, and in time he began to look at her in judgment. It was clear that he no longer thought her innocent and now saw her as someone stirring up a fight.

Time had passed since the marriage, and Beilah had not yet conceived. She had not found happiness in her married life, and Yekutiel's stories had become repetitive. If she at least had a little son, she could find consolation in him. And as much as she wept and begged her husband for a miracle, it didn't help her.

"You help everyone, and many women conceived because of you. But why don't you help me?" she complained.

"You have to make amends," he told her. "You have to ask Jacob Isaac, The Jew, to forgive you for speaking badly of him and accusing him of acts he claims he never committed. I can't help you with that. Go to The Jew and ask him to help."

It was difficult for Beilah to turn to The Jew for assistance. Nevertheless, she asked to meet with him and implored him to pray that she be granted a son. The Jew told her:

"If you promise me that from now on, you will not cooperate with the gossipmongers, who defame me in the ears of my rabbi, I will help you. Not only will you stop telling their lies to the rabbi," he added, "you must promise me that you will not enable them to say good or bad things to you."

She promised, and within a few months she was pregnant and within a year was cradling a son in her arms. She did not know that the weakness of his aging father had been passed on to the boy. She also saw that her husband, The Seer, was shocked when he looked at the forehead of his infant son because he could tell he would not live for long. His hair was black, like hers, and his eyes were a luminous blue. Meir Shalom, she called him, and loved bouncing him up high in her arms and peering into his eyes. From infancy he would stare at her with the utmost love and admiration, as if to say, "I could not wish for a more perfect mother than you."

Her love of the child and attending to his needs filled Beilah's life and spirit, and she felt grateful for the motherhood his birth had given her, and therefore, took care to uphold her promise to The Jew. Whenever anyone wanted to malign The Jew, she immediately changed the subject and did not allow him to finish what he was saying. But when the child grew up and was already three years old, Beilah forgot her promise. Meanwhile, Yekutiel succeeded in entering the court of The Jew of Peshischa, where he heard, according to him, that the followers of The Jew listen to his teachings and whisper among themselves how good and true the words of The Jew are, and what a shame it is that the Rabbi of Lublin does not listen to his words. If he had heard, he would have understood that there was no one better suited to inherit his position than The Jew.

The Jew's followers denied the words of the informer. They swore that The Jew had never made such a claim to succeed The Seer. What they said was completely different. They claimed that if the Rabbi of Lublin were to hear how The Jew spoke about him, he would see how much love was in his words and would never again believe such libelous tales. But the words were not explained to Beilah in this way. It is said that Yekutiel was punished for the lies he told and for the fiery disagreement he ignited, but that Beilah believed him since she had no way of knowing she had been tricked and thus repeated the stories to The Seer. And even if there was no truth to the stories, it could not be denied that The Jew had indeed set up a court for himself and gathered followers of his own in Peshischa, some of whom undoubtedly would have remained followers of The Seer. And despite the fact that there is nothing new under the sun, and the details are known – since, after all, The Seer himself left the court of Rabbi Elimelech and set up a court of his own in Lancut, causing great pain to Rabbi Elimelech until he was forced to move further away to the large city of Lublin – nevertheless, The Seer's anger was aroused against The Jew and he tried to distance himself from him. The libelous stories added fuel to the flames of his anger. Despite that, The Jew didn't give up and continued visiting Lublin, making Beilah even angrier. She would have preferred not to see him since his well-built, attractive appearance reminded her each time anew how much she disliked her aging husband. But it was clear that he, The Jew, had no fear of evil tongues and their influence since he was faithful to his own truth, and no man or object would move him from his path. He would even say:

"The moment a man finds a worthy rabbi for himself, he will not give him up for all the world's wealth because he learns everything from him – from things about the supernal realms to those from this world; even how to fall asleep at night, I learned from my rabbi."

He admired his rabbi and continued to be a follower of The Seer, even though many were puzzled by it. It has already been told that Ironhead, who was firmly opposed to Hassidism, expressed this openly. However, The Jew believed that he could only learn from his rabbi, The Seer – not scriptural innovations, in which The Seer did not excel, but in the mazes of the supernal worlds.

And then, Meir Shalom fell ill. The fever attacked him, his eyes were closed even when he was awake, and his small body trembled. When Beilah understood in her despair that salvation would not come from The Seer, she rushed to Peshischa. She promised The Jew that she would not speak ill of him, and he acquiesced to her request, laid his hand on little Meir Shalom's forehead, and prayed for his recovery. Beilah stared at him, and it was clear to see the doubt on her face. The Jew didn't light candles, didn't give her a talisman, and didn't even open a Torah scroll and read from it as The Baal Shem Tov was wont to do, as she had heard.

But Meir Shalom stopped shaking, opened his eyes, and smiled at her.

As the days went by, Beilah's wrath reappeared once more, and she again spoke badly of The Jew to The Seer. Since she broke her word and drove a wedge between the two great lights, she aroused the anger of the heavens and the boy fell ill again. Once more, Beilah turned, first to The Seer – her husband – to perform a miracle that would cure the boy, and again, he told her, "It's not in my hands, only in the hands of The Jew."

"The boy is burning up," Beilah told her husband. "Your son, ours, that we saw after waiting so long, please..."

But The Seer insisted that he was unable to influence what would happen.

"You didn't keep your promise to The Jew, so only he can save him."

Beila hurried and entered Meir Shalom's room, adjusted the blanket to ease the shivering that shook his little body, stroked his burning cheeks, kissed his forehead, and ran out to the carriage she had ordered in advance and hurried to Peshischa. She went all the way there, herself. She did not send her request with a courier or a messenger. She ordered the carriage driver to whip the horses to gallop faster so they wouldn't arrive too late.

The Jew did not keep her waiting, forgave her, and again prayed for her son's recovery. Another year passed, and again she broke her word. Meir Shalom got sick once more, and again she heard her husband say that she must ask for forgiveness from The Jew. But this time, when she traveled to Peshischa to plead for her son, The Jew refused the request of The Seer's wife, and I could hardly believe my ears.

"How were you able to do that?" I asked.

"The actions of humans determine everything, even

matters of life and death. Beilah promised me repeatedly to stop all her slandering but was unable to overcome her evil inclination…"

"But what is the child guilty of?"

And he explained to me what was involved in interfering with people's fate.

"Ever since the destruction of the Temple, the angels in the heavens above do the work of men, of the Cohens and Levis," he said. "The angels make sacrifices with gold fire tools and burn incense because humans can no longer per-form those chores. When I ask to save a child, I must dis-turb the Angel Raphael from his rest and all his other tasks to free himself in the heavens above to heal the child. And I cannot bother him repeatedly and disturb his Godly work each time Beilah returns to her bad habits."

And I said that they sacrificed the child on the altar.

"No," The Jew proclaimed, "it was known that the child Meir Shalom would not live long. The Seer himself also knew that from the day of his birth. He never spoke about it directly, but I remember what they say when a soul re-turns to the world to rectify something. And when the rectification of the soul has been fulfilled, it returns to the supernal world of truth. Children who die are reincarnated from souls of righteous people who need only a short time to make amends."

The child died, and I understood that Beilah would hate my Jacob Isaac forever and that his rabbi, The Seer, would never forgive him because even if it was written that this would come to pass, everyone knows that it is always possi-ble to change. That is what The Jew said repeatedly – that with complete faith a man can revive the dead, turn silver into gold, and change the ways of nature, and he had already proved it again and again with his ability to heal the sick. Still, in order not to distract the Angel Raphael from his work and to teach the woman a lesson, the little boy died. His mother, as gullible as she may have been, will never again be able to hold him or gaze again at the blueness of his eyes that tell her how perfect she is. I understood Beilah's and The Seer's anger and I justified their unwillingness to forgive because I always thought that benevolence and mercy were more important than the principles of justice and law.

A TALE OF A SICK BOY
AND PIPE TOBACCO

Four Jewish Brides.

The four of them are dressed in white. Four beautiful young, happy brides. Four smiling, laughing brides. A soft light illuminates them.

Two of them stand, the third is seated, and the fourth leans over her. They are preoccupied with themselves and unaware of what is happening around them. Their white clothes are no more than shrouds. White shrouds, some of which have crumbled. The four form a circle and start dancing, and their movements resemble floating.

Sheindel enters the circle again, this time alone, and she turns to me and says, "I, Sheindel, will continue telling you the story of my life with The Jew."

And so Sheindel told me:

As I already told you, it was hard to live with a man who lives with ideals that demand more and more from himself all the time and who dedicates his life and the lives of those close to him to an unattainable goal that he identifies with worshipping God. The Jew not only wholeheartedly believed that he was obliged to dedicate his life to the work of the Creator, he also believed in the goodness to be found in everyone who crosses his path, in every man – even if he is simpler than he, and lower in spiritual standing than he. Even if he is the least of the least, he would find good qualities in him.

He was a genius. And his disciples clung to him because they knew how great his wisdom and learning were. But he himself held that he did not manage to get to a real understanding of things and did not really and honestly know their meaning and origins. Therefore he was modest, minimized his importance, and was satisfied with little. For that reason, he would give more than he could afford to help his fellowmen, and to the extent that he denied himself in order to help others, he ended up in a conflict with his rabbi – Rabbi Jacob Isaac of Lublin.

A seemingly poor man came and asked him for a shirt, saying that he was terribly cold and didn't have suitable clothing; without hesitation, The Jew took off the shirt he was wearing and gave it to the poor man. It was the shirt he had received as a gift from his rabbi, The Seer of Lublin! The same "poor" man, who was nothing more than a swindler, strutted around the streets of Lublin, boasting that he had sold the shirt for a fortune because he knew it wasn't just an ordinary shirt of a holy man, but the shirt that The Holy Jew received from The Seer of Lublin! He boasted about his shrewdness, The Jew's naïveté, and the ease with which he had fooled him.

However, in the action of The Jew, there was more than innocent faith, giving charity, and helping others. Some also saw it as a disregard for the dignity of his rabbi. And the rabbi was also offended by this.

In fact, there was another point to consider in The Jew's being satisfied with very little, and foregoing physical pleasures – because it implied that we, too, the members of his family – should make do with the least of the least and forego the physical pleasures, even with regard to everything connected to food and drink. The food itself, The Jew believed, was not intended for pleasure, so in order not to enjoy it even a little, he would add unnecessary amounts of salt to his food.

As a result, we were all thin. It was forbidden to eat more than was necessary to survive. The food was not intended for carnal pleasure, but to preserve life itself and no more than that. That was how we lived, and that is how we raised the children – to enrich the spirit and despise the matters of the body. And as he was cautious with a person who invested time and effort in caring for his body, so was he full of compliments and praise for those who developed their spirits and mounted to the highest heavenly realms.

He would tell the children the tale of the potatoes and the melody, something that really happened to him and his son Yerachmiel, who accompanied him on one of his journeys. The long trip was made even more arduous by the heavy snow that impeded the horses' progress and blinded them with its bright whiteness. After many hours, they were left without food or drink. When they reached one of the villages, they went into the house of a Jew. His wife served them a bowl of steaming hot potatoes. Yerachmiel was hungry and quickly ate a lot of them. The Jew got angry with him, and the following day, when they continued on their way, he wanted to punish him and ordered him to sit beside the driver and not in the coach. It was very cold, but The Jew insisted. Yerachmiel did not argue. Whenever he came up against his father's ironclad, uncompromising will, he would look down and accept his reprimands with love.

And so Yerachmiel took his place beside the driver, covered his legs with the driver's fur blanket, and began to sing. How delightful the melody was to The Jew; as he listened to his son's voice, he felt the holiness rising and purifying their way of its impurities. In his mind's eye, he envisaged the Gates of Heaven opening in response to his son's singing, canceling the evil decrees and shrouding the whole world in a measure of mercy. And thanks to that melody, they traveled faster, and at their journey's end found themselves on Shiroka Street, where the Torah Study Center of The Seer was located. The Jew praised Yerachmiel for his songs but always reminded him of his unmannerly eating because the act of eating, so he said, must be addressed like an act of holiness. It is not intended to satisfy bodily pleasure, and if a man eats with excessive intent, he can help angels in their work.

And he had another principle: He would not perform miracles. The Seer of Lublin was ready to perform miracles whenever he wished, whereas The Jew believed in worshipping God through studying. Yes, he could perform miracles. So what? Almost anyone can, but it was not his way. And although it was not his way, his righteousness was so great that sometimes he unintentionally performed miracles without having willfully decided to do so. On one of his trips to Lublin, he stopped overnight at a roadside inn on the way. In the morning, he asked to pay for his stay. But the landlord refused and replied that if The Jew insisted on giving something in lieu of paying for his lodging, he would be happy to accept a blessing from him instead. The Jew consented and blessed the innkeeper and his family members, but when he boarded the coach and intended to continue on his way, he heard them calling him back to the house urgently because he hadn't blessed one of the innkeeper's daughters. The Jew got angry and retorted, "So why are you bothering me? Can't she show a little respect and come to my coach so I can bless her."

The Jew did not know that the girl had suffered from paralysis for years and could not walk, but at his command, the girl got up and walked on her own two feet to the carriage and received his blessing. And here, just with his power of speech, and even unintentionally, The Jew healed the patient, and she got to her feet.

When this event became known, many people went and stood at the entrance to our house and asked The Jew to have mercy on them and cure them and their relatives of their ills. Men, women, and children stood waiting for two or three days in the yard in the hope that The Jew would bless them with full recovery or with fertility. But The Jew refused to do so, although it was within his power to show mercy to so many people. He had not only the power to show them mercy, but us, too, because in those days we knew need, poverty, and hunger, and it is accepted that people who come to seek health and a living contribute generously when their wishes are fulfilled. But The Jew, despite all the supplications, refused – he was simply not prepared to perform miracles. And I thought to myself: If a man can perform a miracle and have a good influence on people far from him, then how much more of the same should he do for those close to him . . . Why wouldn't he do that?

Except that The Jew was faithful to his principles and thus his refusal to perform miracles applied to the members of his household themselves, since a man of principles has to be a personal example. So when my little Asher'el, my beloved son, became sick with pneumonia, his father refused to perform a miracle to cure him. In the meantime, the child was very ill. His fever rose, and at times he hallucinated from it. The Jew – his father – for his principles, insisted that he does not perform miracles. I sat beside the child for hours, trying to reduce his fever, and I wrapped snow that I collected at the front door in a kitchen towel, bound it around his forehead, and laid it on his chest. The temperature would not go down, and I had difficulty persuading the boy to drink a little hot soup – only the liquid of the soup – since he had been unable to swallow the noodles for days. He began hallucinating that he was in the room with the teacher and was reciting, in a frail voice, the Torah portion they had learned. Then he hallucinated playing outside with his friends, laughing about something. His speech wasn't clear anymore, and I didn't understand what was so funny to him. I talk to him, but he doesn't answer; he's alone in his own world, although when I press his hand, he responds with pressure, and somehow that calms me. After a few hours he loses consciousness and lies in the bed, burning up from the temperature of his body, as heat spasms plague the little body of my beloved son, and I can't do anything to help…

I ran to the Beit Midrash just as I was, without a coat and my feet in slippers. I burst into where The Jew was teaching. I stood before him and begged him to perform a miracle, to heal the boy.

"It's a sin not to help!" I said. "It's a crime not to save a life. Perform a miracle now and save my son." The students looked at him, and I felt that they understood my heart and wanted their rabbi to help, but nothing helped. The Jew remained true to his principles, even if they would cost him his son's life.

"There is this way and another," he told me. He does not judge those who perform miracles. It is a choice.

"I am talking to you about my son, and you answer me in slogans," I said.

He looked at me with pity and replied, "But I believe in this, Sheindel. I'm not making excuses. That is how I live. Who knows that better than you?"

"You could have saved my beloved sister, and you did nothing. Now, you can save your son, and you're not doing anything. I will stay here, in the Beit Midrash. I won't move, I don't want to be at home when my son's soul passes on…"

I stood stuck to the spot and wept. There was silence in the hall; only the sounds of my weeping were heard. I was cold, and a terrible fatigue took hold of me. I sat on the floor, and my weeping quietened. Only my tears continued flowing soundlessly. He stared at me, and an idea suddenly occurred to him. Charity can save from death! And keeping a commandment in a way that is beyond the limitations of human nature is an omen for being saved in a manner that is also supernatural. If I give charity wholeheartedly, and I agree to give everything I own to the poor, perhaps that will save the life of the child. I agreed. Of course I agreed. What do I care about possessions when I have a chance that my son will be saved? I went to the house that I built, that I saved coins one by one to build, and I sold it, including all its contents, even the bed where the boy lay, and I laid him on a blanket on the cold floor.

I gave away everything, as well as all the money and food that was in the house, and shared it with the poor – with the poor and the drunks, it made no difference. And I gave my Sabbath clothes to the fund for poor brides and went back to him just as I was, and told him that I had sold everything and given the money away. I gave up everything for the child to get well.

He looked up from the book he was reading, stared at me briefly, and said, "You forgot to sell the window frames of the house."

So I sold them, and the house was freezing cold, but Asher recovered. He prayed for his son to get well, and my child was alive. He was weak and sallow, and the house was freezing, but just then The Preacher of Koznitz came to our house to call on Jacob Isaac. He suggested taking Asher'el home with him to recuperate and grow stronger. I agreed. I was fond of The Preacher, who was like a father to me. He had inherited his courageous heart from Rabbi Elimelech of Lizhensk, and I knew he would care for the child with love. I also knew that he had moved to Zelichow to get away from the criticism he faced from those who opposed him in Koznitz, accusing him of negligence for not having time for learning for even one hour a month because he busied himself healing the sick, blessing women, and raising the spirits of sinners. They called him "*Wunder Doktor*," and in my situation, I respected his devotion to the needy and hoped that if there was a deterioration in the child's condition, he would take care of him.

Before their departure, The Preacher sat with me and said, "The time has come to change the boy's name, and from today his name will be Yehoshua Asher. We will keep the name Asher after the name of the father of our *Heiliger* (Holy), our '*Holy Yod*.'"[18] That's what he called Jacob Isaac, my husband, "the Holy Yod," but another name will be added to him as a blessing for a long life." And when I asked him, "Why Yehoshua?" he didn't answer. And I checked it out and found that Moses changed the name of Hoshua Bin Nun to Yehoshua; they interpreted it as "God will save you from the counsel of spies," since the spies were eminent, important people. And I thought to myself that perhaps The Preacher knows something; perhaps the anger of The Seer caused the serious illness, and he wanted to save the child from the Seer's advice.

The separation from my beloved Yehoshuah Asher'el was difficult for me, although I knew that his chances of recovery were better at The Preacher's house. But how difficult it is to part with your child – even when you think that doing so will save his life – both because of the healing powers of The Preacher and the increased distance from the anger and eye of The Seer. The Seer felt strong and heroic with my Jacob Isaac as his rabbi, but I knew that with The Preacher – who was his senior and was named Israel after the Baal Shem Tov, who had blessed his parents with a son, and many called him by the name – The Second Baal Shem Tov – The Seer would not dare to get into a conflict with him. I told myself that I had done everything for his recovery and I could finally breathe. So let him travel and recuperate at The Preacher's home, even if it meant being far away from me.

---

18. The tenth letter of the Hebrew alphabet is the letter *yod*, which is also the first letter of the Hebrew word for Jew, "Yehudi."

And indeed, The Preacher loved Yehoshua Asher and took care of him as if he were his grandson. Each evening he would tell the boy a bedtime story and stay with him until he fell asleep, and before he went to bed, he would check on his sleep and whether he had a fever. One night, when he saw that the boy was sleeping restlessly, he decided to transfer the boy to his room so that he would be able to watch him from close by. And thus the souls of Yehoshua Asher and The Preacher grew so close that when he grew up, he decided to make his home in Zelichow.

And I knew, and knew very well, that The Preacher wanted to keep my Yehoshua Asher far away from Peshischa because of the anger of The Seer. The cause of his anger was obvious: when Meir Shalom, his and his wife Beilah's child, was ill, Jacob Isaac refused to heal him, no matter how much Beilah begged. To him, it was a matter of principle not to perform miracles. And the child died. Ever since then, I did not go to Lublin. Before Meir Shalom's death, I went there once to meet the Rebbetzin, wife of The Seer. I had a pleasant time with her. She received me like a sister, and I, who so yearned for my sister, felt good with her. But since the death of the child, I dared not show my face in Lublin, because how can you go and look into your friend's eyes after your man refused to heal her child? And thus – as a matter of principle – a mother loses her son, and a father loses his son. In this, believe me, The Seer never forgave my Jacob Isaac. Go and live with a righteous man.

And I'll tell you one more thing.

Jacob Isaac often smoked a pipe. His followers said that when The Jew smoked his pipe, he would direct intentions to move matters in the supernal worlds. There are those who exaggerated and compared his pipe-smoking to the intentions of the High Priest in burning incense on the Day of Atonement in the Holiest of Holies, the inner sanctum of the Holy Temple. And so every day, before going to bed for the night, the servant of The Jew would check whether he had enough pipe tobacco to smoke. One day he found The Jew brooding and caught up in a reverie of ideas; hesitating lest he disturb him, he went to bed. In the middle of the night, The Jew woke him and ordered him to go out and buy tobacco. The servant went and returned to tell The Jew that all the shops were closed. Jacob Isaac paced up and down, and back and forth, like a caged lion. There wasn't a corner in the house that he didn't search. He opened all the drawers and all the closets, but in vain. The apologetic servant told him,

"It's a pity that you didn't tell me hours ago. I would have bought you tobacco, and now you would have something to smoke."

"Don't have regrets," The Jew said. "If I want I will have tobacco to smoke, and what's more, the tobacco will come all the way here to me."

Suddenly there was a knock on the door, and standing there was a young fellow, the bridegroom of the neighbor, whose wife had recently given birth to a son and who lived right next door. He immediately turned to Jacob Isaac in tears.

"My son is burning with fever. Please pray for him to recover."

"Do you perhaps have a little tobacco?"

The young man stared at him in amazement.

"I don't smoke, I'm sorry."

"Search through all your pockets. Who knows? Maybe you'll find some."

The young man did not understand what was so important about tobacco when his son was so feverish. Nevertheless, he did not want to anger the righteous man at this hour lest his prayer for the child be filled with resentment. He put his hand in his pocket and found a pouch full of tobacco. He looked at the pouch in his hand in amazement and understood that instead of taking his pouch of money, he had taken the one in which his father-in-law kept his smoking paraphernalia.

"I apologize. I will run home right away and bring my wallet," he said.

Jacob Isaac laughed, looked at his servant, and said, "This is better."

Of course he prayed for the child's recovery. The child benefitted from the prayer of a righteous man at little cost – the price of which was some tobacco. Undoubtedly, a miracle had taken place and it didn't require an argument to consider whether it was right, if it served the principle and the way, and whether the seeker was worthy of a miracle, or if it is necessary to sell everything you possess. I'm not judging; I'm just reporting what occurred.

That's what Sheindel told me.

And I listen to her story and notice a change in her posture, body language, and how she stares at me. Her gaze is open, and it is clear that the hesitation and confusion at the beginning of her marriage have been replaced over the years with self-assurance and even determination.

With a slight gesture, she rearranges the train of her dress. Clearly, she is a woman who takes care of her appearance.

133

Years later she will ask her son to buy her some fashionable spectacles on a trip to Lemberg. She could still not be considered beautiful, but there is something elegant about the impression she makes. She is stem-like. Tall and slender. Her hair is tied back with a scarf; not a single strand peeps out, God forbid, so no one can say that she is wanton, because it is well known that a woman who goes out in public with her hair wild and uncovered is liable to divorce without the alimony settled on in her *ketuba*.[19] A woman covering her hair is one of every Jewish home's most important tenets; she who proudly displays her hair beckons invitingly to poverty and strange troubles to befall her husband and children.

The outsiders led by Lilith also flaunt their hair. While even when she sleeps, Sheindel's hair is covered with a kerchief, and only on Sabbath does she adorn it with a beautiful brooch.

19. A ketubah is a Jewish marriage contract. It is considered an integral part of a traditional Jewish marriage, and outlines the rights and responsibilities of both parties.

THE SECRET OF THE PORPHYRA

Sheindel continues her story.

After Asher'el recuperated, our lives returned to their routine. With the passing of the years, I had learned to say what was in my heart. I gave up keeping silent, which might be why I became known as a "bad woman." Anyway, all around us the Torah scholars were speaking dreadfully about women, even if they were not talkative or fixed in their opinions. Even My Jew used to do that. One Shabbat, he told his students about a Hassid who came into the Court of Heaven. Many had praised him for his honesty, and the court was already considering accepting him into heaven, but suddenly an angel came and reported on something terrible that he had done. The angels were astounded and asked him why he had behaved that way.

"My wife caused me to do that," he said.

The angel laughed. Couldn't the Jew find a better excuse? Was it really possible that his wife caused him to commit that sin? The Heavenly Court decided to punish the Hassid for his transgression. Regarding the angel who laughed at him, it was decided that he would be sent down to earth for another incarnation, during which he would take a wife, and let's see how he manages with a woman of his own. All the students who heard the story laughed out loud, but I, who listened attentively, was insulted to the depths of my soul. Tears welled up in my eyes. Is that what my husband thinks of women in general, and me in particular? Because I heard them say that I was a wicked wife to The Jew and that he would face especially difficult tests because of me, and through them he would be purified, refined, and rise to higher levels of sanctity.

More than once, The Jew and I fought, principally about matters associated with making a living. I was always quick to anger, while The Jew always said of himself that he was never angry, but since he knew that in order to overcome anger, one had to have a good fight from time to time, and he would stage disagreements to enable me to fight as one should and give vent to my anger. What a wonderful human being, no? A man who is bereft of anger...

But try and think what it really is like to live with such a perfect man, an angel of a man, who is certain that he is always right, and out of the kindness of his heart allows you to unburden your feelings.

Once I went to visit Rivka, the wife of Rabbi Bunim, the pharmacist. Rivka told me what her husband told her about a particular fight between me and The Jew. And this, she told me, is what Simcha Bunim told her:

"Once, when I sat with The Jew in the Beit Midrash, and we quibbled about the rights of a divorced woman to the total value of her premarital marriage agreement's financial settlement, through the window we saw Sheindel approaching like a storm. Despite the terrible cold outside – or perhaps because of it – her cheeks were flaming red, and her steps were so rushed that she appeared to hover above the frozen ground. Her headcovering tilted slightly to the side, and since she always put it on so meticulously, we knew that she was really upset this time. She burst into the room, ignoring everyone sitting there, and her gray eyes stared at The Jew without blinking. Her piercing, feverish gaze showed how angry she was.

"I cannot go on like this. There is no money in the house, and the children must eat. I am ashamed to go to the market and again ask for credit that I'll pay back later."

"Yesterday you appeared here with exactly the same complaint, and you saw for yourself. I returned home at noon with all the groceries necessary for the meal…"

"Because, today, too, I don't have the means to buy anything. You're right, yesterday there was that Jew who asked you to find a cure for his sick daughter…"

The Jew interrupted his wife angrily.

"I don't invent cures!" he said. "You know very well that I don't deal in miracles. I agreed to pray for her recovery, and he left me a note with the girl's name and also a few groszy…"

"A few groszy? There were more than enough *gilden* and had you given them to me, they would have been enough until the new month. But the moon had barely risen in the sky, and you rushed to the market and gave away almost all the money to the poor women in the market."

The Jew's forehead grew firm. "You know very well that I do not allow money to lie fallow at home overnight! How can one hold the money to no purpose overnight when children are starving? Would you like children to be left without food even when you have the ability to help them?"

Her cheeks reddened, and the effort she was making not to scream was clearly visible. She clenched her teeth until white marks were visible on her cheeks. But she could not control herself.

"But that's exactly the problem when you never leave a coin at home! Every day it's the same story…"

"And don't you think it's better to only worry about that day? Or do you prefer that children go to sleep hungry? Do you think the children of the poor women who go looking for scraps of cabbage or some rotten potatoes in the market at the end of the day don't deserve to go to bed on a full stomach? Of course, I would go out and give them any coin I have in my pocket…"

"You always do that. You preach morals and insist that you are right. Meanwhile, *our* children are hungry!"

"It isn't evening yet. Don't worry – they won't die of hunger!"

Sheindel turned her back on him and left the room. As she left, her steps were slow, her head was bowed, and despite not getting what she asked for, it was obvious that she was less agitated than when she arrived.

"When the argument began," Simcha continued his story, "I diminished my presence by withdrawing to the corner of the table and barely breathed. Yet the stormier the argument became, the more I grew surprised and astounded. I had never seen The Jew so angry, and after his wife departed, he turned to me, smiling.

I asked him, "What was that? I have never seen you angry. To tell the truth, your reactions were exaggerated… after all, it's possible to understand Sheindel, and it isn't easy, you know, to begin all over again every day…"

But The Jew interrupted me with a smile.

"I wasn't angry. Anger is a stranger to me. But I felt that

138

she was furious and needed to release her feelings. That's why I responded and disagreed with her. She needed this argument."

Rivka finished telling me Simcha Bunim's story and had a good laugh. I kept my thoughts to myself. I could not stop thinking about the son of The Seer. If my husband really never got angry, as he insists to himself, and anger was so foreign to him, why was he so strict with Beilah?

And while Rivka was already talking about another matter, I thought about my husband's strange habits. After all, he also behaved with awful strictness toward his students, and the more talented the student was, the tougher he was with him. He was also especially strict with his firstborn, Yerachmiel, and one could sense genuine anger in him if his son's answer didn't please him. Was he then also pretending to be angry?

I suddenly recalled an event that took place with Asher, the father of The Jew, shortly after I married him. He was then the presiding judge of the court in Przedborz where they brought a case against him for declaring a chicken kosher after some doubts had been raised. The objectors claimed that the chicken was not kosher and fined him heavily. The Jew traveled to the city of his birth and spent two months studying with the people there until it became clear to them all that his father had been right about the chicken being kosher. But then he stayed and continued studying with them for another two months, and it turned out in the intense discussion that the chicken had indeed been *treif*.

He told them, "In a long-winded debate, we can reach one conclusion on one occasion, and quite the opposite conclusion on another. So it was a miscarriage of justice that you did not accept his Halachic[20] ruling."

They immediately repaid the fine to Rabbi Asher.

In truth – as I also knew – my husband did not consider the memorization of the Halacha or its rulings to be the most important aspect of Judaism. Most of the time, he and his students were concerned with the supernal worlds and not with what was happening here and now, out of a deep conviction that every action we make in this world, good or bad, affects what happens in all the other realms, and what happens there is much more important than what occurs here, in this world, which is no more than a corridor. Therefore, out of devotion to the fate of all the worlds, he insisted on keeping to his principles.

And I knew there was another side to him: He was not always so observant and difficult. There are creatures with whom his heart is merciful. As opposed to The Seer, he never feared conversing with women and would turn to talk to them on the street and in the market. He had no fear of not being able to control his libido without placing restrictions on himself. Don't rush to the conclusion that he believed that women weren't inferior to men, but because he had a measure of respect for them, he would make time to also converse with women about matters that were not the loftiest of life on the world's agenda, although he may have done so, thinking that the very act of dealing with simple and carnal matters might raise the sparks of holiness trapped within them. And of course, he was always willing to give

---

20. Halacha is the collective body of Jewish religious laws that are derived from the written and oral Torah.

charity and indeed never left money overnight in his home. He considered charity to be an important principle. As he repeatedly reminded me, charity saves us from death and has the power to ameliorate judgments reached in the highest realms. Still, it also has great importance in our world because it saves children from hunger and cold. And he was always convinced that even if he dispersed all his money, it wouldn't harm our family. His faith was always unlimited, and he believed that the Almighty, Blessed be He, would take care of our worldly needs on that day.

In the early years of our marriage, I slept with him in one room. We had two beds, and we slept apart; each bed was against a different wall.

Winter came, and we didn't have groszy to heat the house. Jacob Isaac went to the market and stopped at the counter of Ethel, the widow, who sat with her little daughter on a low stool and stared at the falling flakes of snow.

"Go home, Ethel," my husband told her.

"No, I'm staying here," she told him.

"What's there for me to do at home? Look for yourself. All the goods are standing on the counter in my stall. On such cold days, there is no demand for the shining hairpins I sell. But that's all I have to offer. I bought them cheap and thought that perhaps people would buy them because they were a bargain at the price. Look at her." She pointed at her daughter. "See how beautiful and shimmering she looks with these pins in her braids."

Just then The Jew noticed the little girl curled up and snuggling close to her mother. She was small and scrawny, and wore a thin coat, with two fair braids and huge blue eyes sunken in their sockets with black rings that showed her fatigue and poor nutrition. Clips with sparkling stones stuck on them with unpracticed hands so that the heavy layer of glue on the black metal clip was visible. Had the girl been plump and smiling, perhaps people would have been tempted to buy the hairclips with which she adorned herself.

But with such an anguished face, who feels like making themselves look beautiful? Although she cuddled up to her mother and clung to her as best she could, the girl trembled like a blown leaf.

"It's cold, Ethel. Be careful that the little one doesn't get sick. Go home."

"No. As soon as I get home, the children immediately want me to put together a meal for them. I don't want to. And this little one hasn't eaten a thing during this whole long, exhausting day."

"Here, Ethel." He handed her coins from his pocket. "Take these few coins for dinner. Hurry and buy cabbage and cook some hot soup for your children. Do you have coal to light a fire?"

"I have coal," she nodded.

"Go quickly now, Ethel. Your children are waiting at home."

"I don't beg for coins. Be kind and take these two pins to decorate your wife's headscarf on the Sabbath."

And after he gave all his money to Ethel, there was none left to buy coal to warm his own house. At night, Jacob Isaac hurriedly pushed his bed close to mine and embraced me with his left arm beneath my head and his right arm around me. I snuggled up to him, maybe out of wakefulness, maybe out of sleep, pressed against the warmth of his body, and he gently caressed my face until he, too, fell asleep.

My sleep was sweet and pleasant, and I sank into a dream. In it, we are both in white linen nightgowns. We stand in a hall full of illuminating sparks, a radiant world through which a river of bright light flows and illuminates all its surroundings with precious light. Jacob Isaac converses with figures who appear to be the souls of righteous men, and they are differently and strangely dressed. They are deep in lively conversation; angels interfere in the discussion every now and then, and wondrous singing is heard around them. Jacob Isaac turns to an image on a high seat with a magnificent face. The figure is dressed in a kind of blue cloak with many bloodstains, on which are embroidered the names of Jews who died for the sanctification of God's name. The name of Jacob Isaac is also on the cloak, and we watch and see a spectacle of galloping horses that almost trample Jacob Isaac under their hooves. I shout a loud, bitter cry:

"Stop the horses! Immediately! Where's Rabbi David? Let him come and save us! He has to speak to the horses and make them stop running!"

Jacob Isaac, awakened by my screaming, calmed me down, and when I asked what was that Porphyra that lent the cape its color, he understood that I had joined him in the rising of his soul because I had never heard of that snail whose sea-blue color is used to color the cape of the High Priests.

It may happen that people closely connected to one another dream the same dreams.

When they are dreaming, their souls leave their bodies and wander to different places, and sometimes they clasp the hand of a sister soul and visit other realms. A person may sometimes be alone, or sometimes with someone close to him, and sometimes it is possible that the two of them will unite with one another.

As a result of the dream, I thought that closeness between me and The Jew was imminent. And I began to take an interest in the spiritual questions he dealt with. In the evenings, I sat and listened. The lights went out, the shops closed, the market square emptied, and the children were asleep in their beds. I sat with my sewing tools to mend what needed fixing. I was fond of this work because it didn't require deep concentration, and I was able to listen to Jacob Isaac teaching in the adjacent room. His lessons were fascinating. People would listen to his words even through the chimney on the roof, and sometimes even the souls of the dead would come and hear him. And I had the privilege of hearing what he was saying from inside my room. I thought about how much I would like to make the time to hear things from the Torah and listen and study, instead of running around all day. And here, the opportunity to listen and learn things from the Torah had been given to me, not only at night but also on Sabbath evenings, when the Torah scholars sat around the table. With the help of my daughters, I prepared the Sabbath meals after running around between the stalls in the markets to buy all that was required for the meals. And between serving up the food and passing the dishes to the students so that, God forbid, I wouldn't wander around among the guests, I would listen to the words of the Torah while sitting in my room or from the kitchen, feeling my soul moving closer to the soul of Jacob Isaac, My Jew, and perhaps the time of love between us had arrived.

THE GATE OF LOVE

Four Jewish Brides.

The four of them are dressed in white. Four beautiful, young, happy brides. Four smiling, laughing brides. A soft light illuminates them.

Two of them stand, the third is seated, and the fourth leans over her. They are preoccupied with themselves and unaware of what is happening around them. Their white clothes are no more than shrouds. White shrouds, some of which have crumbled. The four form a circle and start dancing, and their movements resemble floating.

Sheindel enters the circle again, turns to me, and says: "I, Sheindel, will tell you about the last year of The Jew's life."

And so Sheindel says:

These were the years of war. Napoleon Bonaparte and his conquests shook the foundations of the world, as it was then. Napoleon asked for Poland's help in his wars, and in compensation promised to return Poland to its former glory. And indeed, in the month of Heshvan/October 1806, the French army conquered considerable Prussian territory, and as the year progressed established the Principality of Warsaw. By July 1807, Napoleon had conquered Austria and annexed large parts of it to the new Polish Principality. A liberal constitution was established in the Principality of

145

Warsaw, and two legislative houses, a lower and an upper one, were established. Serfdom was abolished, and it was determined that all inhabitants would have equal rights and duties, regardless of religion or status. The Jewish intelligentsia hoped that they would also be recognized, and when Napoleon reached Warsaw, they sang his praises for his bravery and statesmanship. But only the enlightened and the assimilated welcomed him with hope. The righteous, the Hassidic leaders among them, The Seer of Lublin, and The Preacher of Kozhnitz, feared that the spirit of freedom and equality of the French Revolution might obscure the spiritual uniqueness of the Jewish people. They feared that the equality of rights and obligations would indeed benefit the Jews economically but would distance them from their Jewishness. They were especially concerned about their children being educated in state schools and their obligation to military service. How would their sons live in military camps? What would they eat? In the end, they would consume treif, would be forced not to keep the Sabbath, and would not have time to learn. The state schools would distance them from learning the Holy Scriptures. Their position on this point grew stronger after demands were heard that the Jews avoid all the outward signs that differentiate between them and the rest of the country's population. They were required to change their clothing, their language, and even their customs. In this way, the righteous feared there would be no more Jews living like Jews. And indeed, because of the influence of The Seer of Lublin and The Preacher of Kozhnitz, the status of equal rights to the Jews was delayed for ten years, from 1806 until 1816; due to their efforts, the Jews were released from military service.

However, the righteous Hassidic leaders of Poland also found some benefits in Napoleon's wars. They believed they were the wars of Gog and Magog that would usher in Redemption, and they worked toward the arrival of the Messiah. Rabbi Zalman of Liadi in Russia, The Preacher of Kozhnitz, and The Seer of Lublin in Poland aligned themselves with the side opposing Napoleon. They wanted to tip the scales against him. If Bonaparte won, Rabbi Zalman of Liadi, the founder of Chabad, reckoned that the wealth of the Jews would increase and their standing in the world would rise, but the Jews would move away from their Jewishness. And if, as opposed to that, Alexander the Emperor of Russia won, the poverty of the Jews would be exacerbated and they would be humiliated, but their connection to Judaism would grow stronger. The three of them did everything they could: they prayed, pursued spiritual intentions, and meditated as they performed unique Kabbalistic rites to promote the victory of the symbol of tyranny, Alexander the Russian. The situation of the Jews under his rule was not good – decrees, persecution, and taxes – but Alexander was a religious man. The honoring of religion, any religion, was important to him. In the opinion of the righteous men, life was better under his rule than the other possibility, which signified equal rights and the dangers of assimilation. Since preference must be given to the spirit over the body, the righteous men believed that the rule of tyranny that had Redemption on its side was preferable to a life without persecution, which was likely to lead to the apostasy of the fundamentals of Judaism. The only one who nevertheless supported Napoleon was Rabbi Menachem Mendel of Rimanov, who saw in Napoleon's wars the war of Gog and Magog and the coming of the Messiah, but also believed in Napoleon's declaration, as he stood before the gates of Jerusalem, that the Jewish homeland was about to arise.

All four of the rabbis devoted themselves to intense magical work in an attempt to shape the course of history. Their purpose was to influence the coming of Redemption in the upper supernal world by influencing the wars in the lower worlds. And their main purpose was to intervene in what was happening with intentions and unifications that would eventually lead to the exit of the Messiah from his supernal temple.

The Jew, on the other hand, decided not to interfere in all this and continued to hold on to his belief that what will bring the Messiah closer are the actions of the followers themselves. Miracles would not bring about Redemption, he maintained – only repentance and righteous acts would. If every Jew will make amends for his private transgressions, as it were, and fully repent, Redemption will follow. Evil is not outside us but inside, within the man. When the Jews learn to love and behave compassionately with one another, then the Messiah will come.

In Tammuz (June) 1812, Napoleon's army invaded Russia. The Russian forces did not resist, but rather drew him deeper into their territory; by the Jewish New Year two months later, a bloody battle took place in Borodino, on the outskirts of Moscow. Oh – then The Seer and The Preacher prayed and worked in the supernal worlds for Napoleon's defeat. Only Rabbi Menachem Mendel of Rimanov prayed for him. It wasn't a simple decision to intervene in the supernal worlds, and it wasn't with ease that The Preacher of

Kozhnitz played his part in the effort. He knew very well that the pangs of the Messiah involve the suffering of many, and if the Messiah comes, it will be preceded by the pangs of the Messiah, that is, the death of many of the children of Israel. But after he was convinced that this was the way, he agreed to join The Seer and Rabbi Zalman of Liadi. The three of them prayed together, each in his place, for the defeat of Napoleon; in the New Year prayers, they focused their intent to influence the supernal realms by blowing the shofar, and on Shabbat, The Preacher and The Seer, each at his location, reading from the Portion of Jethro, altered the words in verse 18 to "Napoleon will fall." During the prayers, they prayed to "annihilate them forever" and "cause division amongst the evildoers." Indeed, following that Shabbat, those prayers, and their deep intent – Napoleon's downfall – began, and the Russian weather froze his army.

A year went by, and again the righteous men wanted to interfere in the course of history. This time they wanted to affect the great battle that was due to take place near Leipzig in 1813. The real battles, The Seer explained, do not take place on the battlefield but in the supernal realms, and the righteous men of the generation are the people who direct the course of the war. But this time, The Seer commanded The Jew to participate in the effort. The Jew surrendered and joined in the battle.

Here, I need to pause in telling the tale of the Napoleonic Wars to say that The Seer had never forgiven My Jew for not saving his son's life. The death of the child was blamed on The Jew, and The Seer sought revenge. He chose to cloak his revenge in a cover of piety. He told The Jew that a unique rectification needed to be made in the supernal worlds, one that would advance the coming of Redemption. He added that such refinement could only be secured by one with especially high standing in the supernal worlds. He directed his words to Jacob Isaac himself, of course. Did he think of covering his intention with flattering remarks? Did he not know there was no return from where he was sending my beloved Jacob Isaac? And My Jew also knew the meaning of these things and what his future held. He looked into the eyes of The Seer, and knew that the Seer, who could also foresee the future, knew that he would not return after completing the task he was imposing on him. When The Jew told me these things, I saw, in my mind's eye, the crooked little smile quivering on the corner of The Seer's mouth: The time to take revenge had come. May the Almighty forgive me for thinking like that. At any rate, My Jew knew that his rabbi had not forgiven him, and he realized the significance of the mission he had been sent to fulfill and began to prepare himself for the impending day.

First, he told me about the four people who entered the orchard.[21] He understood me and knew immediately that I would illustrate the words in my imagination, address them as I saw them in my mind, and treat them as they are — and that is exactly how I'll tell you the story now, not as my man told me, not as it was originally, but as I understood it and as it was pictured in my mind. I pictured the four ascending to the sky and entering the orchard, a heavenly garden

---

21. Four people entered the orchard. The first, Rabbi Akiva, entered in peace and left in peace. The second, Ben Azzai, "looked and died." The third, Ben Zoma, "looked and was hurt (became insane)." The fourth, Elisha Ben Avuya, known as "the other," cut down the plantings (*Hagiga 14,2*). Became a heretic.

full of trees with a magnificent palace at its center. And the palace was built of such shining, smooth marble bricks that they looked like water, like an ice palace. The four climb the stairs of the heavens up to the highest halls, aiming for the Hall of Love. On the upward path they have to choose between light and darkness, between shining marble and tongues of fire flickering in the darkness, because there is not only a palace of light there, but also dangers in the shape of a flashing, twisting sword, and dark palaces standing on the side of the road that beckon and invite the climber to discover the knowledge they contain. The walk of the four in the orchard was also a walk to the end. The road is hard and winding, and chasms of abysses gape in it, and mountains on mountains rise in it, and you have to overcome demons and fears, passions and evil, and impurity. It's easy for a person to be tempted by fire that flares up and to fall into the captivity of evil.

In my mind's eye, I saw how the four-faced forces engulf the soul and pull it to the opposite pole. And I understood that each one of them is drawn to the power at the root of his soul.

Even though Rabbi Akiva warned them and told them, "When you get to the pure marble stones, don't say water," meaning, be careful, don't distort reality, don't let your inner world influence the way you interpret what you will see – the remaining three men were not up to it.

Ben Azzai was young and had not yet married or fathered children. He only glimpsed at the holiness and could not contain it. He looked at it and died. In my imagination, I saw him enter the palace in the sky, lost in the heights of the heavens, overcoming bumpy roads and winding paths; then he opens a door to the hall, looks in, and cannot bear the sight, so he drops straight down and hits the hard ground. The ground has two faces: one of life and the other of death. On the one hand, seeds are buried in it that germinate and grow and turn into nutritious, life-giving food, but on the other, the dead are buried in it because from dust we were created, and to dust we return. And Ben Azzai fell down onto the dust and died, because in the choice between the material roots of the tree of life and the spiritual treetop, Ben Azzai chose the dust. Perhaps his error was his being too young and too enthusiastic, but he was also a great believer. Since the Almighty loved him and his innocent faith, he died before he reached the "other" – Satan and impurity, because in the eyes of the Almighty, death is preferable to falling on the other side.

Ben Zoma was drawn to the spirit. The spirit of the "other" diverted him from the right direction. He was embarrassed and confused by the mess he saw, as witnessed by the fact that the spirit of the other took and led him to the foundation of impurity; because the spirit struck him, he lost his sanity. He looked – and he was struck.

Elisha Ben Avuya was drawn to the dancing tongues of fire, to the burning coals that appeared as torches. Thus he went down in the halls, down the left side, the side of the fire, and there met the other side, the side of impurity, the *Sitra Achra*, and listened to his words about the essence of good and evil because his faith in Divine goodness had long since been shaken. He saw a boy who climbed to the top of a tall tree at his father's command, in order to chase away a dove. An innocent child climbed the tree in order to observe two commandments that promised long life, and at that moment fell and died. And doubts crept into Elisha's heart, and he lost his faith. He believed that there were two inclinations – good and evil – and he did not understand that the Gate of Love is a place with no boundaries, no time and no space, a place where light and darkness, good and evil, first and second, spirit and matter mix. His clear mind did not understand the connections between things, how everything is connected, and how a butterfly flapping its wings on one side of the world causes a hurricane on the other side. Elisha sought to understand the clear and sharp, the bright and understandable. Therefore he was willing to hear the Sitra Achra and agree with what it said; therefore he cut down on the plantings. And he not only sinned in thought but also became a heretic, stopped observing edicts, rode his horse on Shabbat, slept with prostitutes, and identified with the hated rule of Rome.

Only Rabbi Akiva got out safely. He is the only one who stuck to the right side and successfully ascended and reached the Hall of Love because he was a man of love who understood that earthly love is no less than heavenly love. He loved Rachel, the daughter of Ben Kalba Savua, and he also loved God to the extent that he was ready to give his soul for his love of God, and also died for the sanctification of God. Later, when the Romans tortured him and tore his flesh with iron combs, and his pupils asked him how much he was prepared to suffer, he replied,

"All my life, I wrestled with the verse, 'You shall love the Lord, your God, with all your heart and soul,' and I knew that I wasn't observing this as well as I should. Only now, when I am giving up my life, I feel that I am observing the commandment of loving the Creator of the Universe."

And I understood from his words that the success of Rabbi Akiva also led to his death.

My Jew told me the story of the four to prepare me for what was to happen. Their journey to the orchard is connected to the fate of the people of Israel during the rule of the Roman Empire, in the days when the Romans persecuted the Sages of Israel and put many of them to death. While, in our time – the time of The Jew and me – the Napoleonic Wars were being fought, that also threatened to bring great darkness to the story of our nation, to assimilation and extermination, unless the days of the Messiah come, with bright light and Redemption. And like Rabbi Akiva, my beloved Jacon Isaac was called to the highest heavens. Now, The Seer had appointed him to intervene in the heavens in the war about to break out down here and influence its outcome. Who will win – Napoleon or his enemies? A new threatening order or the old familiar regime? And The Seer knew that The Jew would not be burned in the fire or frozen in the snow, or even lose his sanity but, at the same time, he also knew that the odds were great that his soul would be infected with great love, because the Gate of Love is attained through true prayer. There is no prayer truer than that of My Jew. Perhaps I am mistaken about The Seer, and he didn't have evil intent toward him, but he was fully aware of the terrifying danger of entering the Gate of Love.

He knew that The Jew would not be confused, nor would his heart be drawn to the temptations of the "other." He knew that he would reach the Fiftieth Gate, and knew that the significance of it would be death because the Fiftieth Gate is not revealed to any man; it is latent and secret. It is within man's ability to reach forty-nine Gates, but regarding the fiftieth, where the Almighty resides, no man will enter and live to tell about it.

Even Moses entered, but only after he died. And with all that, it is revealed and known that whoever reaches the Fiftieth Gate has the power to cancel edicts and bring on the days of the Messiah, for there, mercy is complete and whole. And this is the mission that The Seer set for my Akiva – meaning my Jacob Isaac – I suddenly mixed up the letters and called him Akiva instead of Jacob[22] to reach the Fiftieth Gate. A mission that means death. My Jacob Isaac knew that and prepared me for his death.

"There are places in the orchard that one does not enter," I said, "There are places where you are lost."

My Jew answered me, "No, I won't lose my way in the orchard. I won't be like Ben Zoma who looked and was hit, and I won't be like Ben Azzai, who stared and died. Like Rabbi Akiva, who succeeded, I will not ask for the root of my soul in the orchard, and I won't look for water." And he fell silent.

"And, don't be like 'The Other,'" I said.

"No, I won't be like 'The Other,' who cut back on the planting. I have great faith," he replied. "I believe it won't diminish. But neither do I know what will become of me," he continued in a tremulous voice.

"For even people of the higher echelons can fall to the depths if they become proud and condescending. This can only be avoided by those who remember their temporal

---

22. Note how the names Jacob and Akiva consist of almost the same Hebrew letters ב ק ע י Ya'akov and Akiva א ב י ק ע.

impermanence compared to God," he continued in his apprehensive voice, "and I have always lived in awe of God. Fright and fear took hold of me every time I prayed because I came to see only the least of His enormous power. It is like someone who walks in a forest where there are dangerous animals, and nothing can be seen in the surrounding darkness. But he knows that there are evil animals in this forest, and he is really afraid. Now, imagine how much that man's fear increases if he suddenly hears a lion roar. His fear doubles or trebles, but he still hopes the lion won't notice him – but . . . oh, dear! In the faint light of the moon between the clouds, he discovers that the lion is just a few steps away from him. Won't his fear increase a thousandfold?

That is precisely how I feel as I mount the heavenly steps when praying. And perhaps that fear will save me. But I don't judge anyone who has met Satan. His tricks are numerous, and his persuasiveness is mighty. I am frightened; you know that, because you have observed me praying. And perhaps this reverence will save me. And if I do succeed, I hope with all my heart that arrogance will not make me fall."

And that same night he told me the story of Rabbi Joseph de la Reina, Joseph of the Queen, who could have been Joseph of the Divine Spirit. But he ended up being Joseph de la Ruina because his pride brought about his downfall. Joseph was a wise, learned man who wanted to bring the Messiah and almost succeeded; he overcame Satan, and tied him in chains. Immediately Satan, Lilith, and their entourage of demons surrounded them, weeping bitterly and mourning their defeat. At that very moment, Joseph wondered in his heart how people would be able to know that he, Joseph, succeeded in bringing the coming of the Messiah and what all those who doubted his power to overcome the devil would say now. He almost brought Redemption, but when these thoughts of pride and vanity passed through his head, the achievement in heaven was annulled, darkness and smoke covered the world, and the opening for the coming of the Messiah was closed. With all his attributes, in the end Rabbi Joseph committed the sin of hubris.

"And I, 1,000 years after that Joseph, have been commanded by The Seer to speed up the coming of the Messiah. But who knows what will be? A man is but a man. But, my beloved, I am unworthy and insignificant. And in any case, the end is already known." He didn't add a word, but I already knew and tears began to roll down my cheeks.

On the eve of the appointed day, he told me, "Tomorrow, when I pray, if you see that my condition is bad, lay your hand on my cheek. I will feel you, and that will ease my journey." And I knew that the time had come because every time My Jew prepared to pray, he would take leave of the children and me as if he would not return. But he had never asked me to lay my hand on his cheek. He would ask me to wake him up if he fainted during the prayer and bring him hot tea and crackers to revive his soul. And, now, suddenly, he has such a strange new request.

"Why?" I asked. "Why do you want me to rest my hand on you?"

He replied,

"Because I aim at the Gate of Love, and if I feel your love, I will reach it." And after a minute he said, "Your love will help me reach the Gate of Love, the 49th level, and from there to the fiftieth, the Gate of Godliness. It requires a very high spiritual level from me. Nobody enters the Fiftieth

Gate," he said, "and even if he does enter, no one returns from there."

He never lied to me, so he did not try to deny anything.

"And after my death, make it known that there was once "A Jew," and he is no more. A simple man, a simple Jew. Tell the stories of that man, and that is how you will make your living."

"A simple and precious Jew," I said.

"Say whatever you want," he told me.

When he prayed the next day, he was seized by a fright and trembling, the likes of which he had never before felt. His spirit was so aroused that his feet dug hard into the floor and made two deep holes in it. He had never reached such a degree of ecstatic devotion. I put my hand on his cheek and my head on his chest, and for a moment he calmed down, a smile lit up his face, and he held my hand and fell asleep. He remained in a deep sleep for three days until he died. And Asher'el, my son, who was beside him, told us that in his last hour, his lips mimed the verses "Let not the foot of pride overtake me,"[23] and "There is none else beside him."[24] His soul left his body and united with God, and I knew that my beloved man had departed this world through his love of the Almighty, and I understood that he had overcome the powers of evil and all the obstacles on the way and had seen the good Lord and clung to him – and God also looked at his face and accepted him into his bosom.

In my mind's eye, I saw the throne. It appeared to be

---

23. Psalms 36,12, Translation *Mechon Mamre Bible*.

24. Deuteronomy, 6.35, Translation *Mechon Mamre Bible*.

made of crystal, and around it was a luminous glow. Rivers of burning fire flowed beneath the throne, and the figure seated on it had the visage of a human sitting and talking about Torah; his shining garment radiated like the sun and was as white as snow. Righteous men sat before him, and the entourage of the heavens above stood on their feet; the sun and the heavenly signs were to his right and the moon and stars to the Almighty's left as he sits and interprets new secrets in the Torah that are to be given by the hand of the Messiah, while My Jew sits there and unravels complicated enigmas.

This is what Sheindel told me. And when she stopped telling her story and fell silent, I think about the Jewish leadership of those times, that in the name of their principles of observing the religion, and not out of mercy, preferred the children of Israel to suffer cruel decrees, pogroms, and blood libels, provided they continue to live in a closed, segregated community.

Moreover, I am still trying to grasp the matter of the stairs and ascending to the celestial spheres. I think of this phenomenon when the heavens open and the sun's rays illuminate layers of sky, a firmament within a firmament, azure within blue. Sometimes such a sight is exposed to me when I'm driving home, leaving Jerusalem for Mevasseret Zion, and on the way the sun's rays suddenly shimmer, and a kind of crown is revealed. This crown opens the heavens and stirs the heart as one continues to gaze, knowing that it is both forbidden and dangerous. It is dangerous not only because of the possibility of a road accident that, heaven forbid, may occur on the twisting road, as even when there is a traffic jam and all the cars are stuck, I warn myself not to glance, not to be tempted, because I am not on the spiritual level worthy of such a sight. Obviously, those who entered the heavens, ascended the stairs and were deserving of it could see what was happening on each firmament – on one there was gold, on the other silver, until they reached the shining mirror, the highest heaven and the abode of the Almighty. But in order to reach that place – the illuminating mirror – the soul has to be pure, as if you are standing in the presence of a sparkling mirror made of crystal and you don't see your image in it because your soul is the observer, not your physical being. And if your soul is completely pure and clean, you can see what is beyond this mirror – the highest worlds.

A few days later I remember that I met The Jew in my dream. We walked on the beach that often appears in my dreams, a beach of coarse, wet, black sand with many paths along it. On one side are stretches of wild nature with small lakes and green vegetation, and on the other are landscapes, construction sites, and high-rise buildings. Actually, The Jew lives in a multi-story building, on the second or third floor. And the two of us, The Jew and I, chatted together. The atmosphere was comfortable and pleasant, as if we were old friends. And I was amazed to discover how young he was. He was dressed as the ultra-religious dress nowadays, but since we were in his home, he was wearing a white shirt and a kind of vest over it, with the sleeves of the shirt rolled up. Suddenly I looked out the window and saw the sea. I went to the veranda that was closed with a white aluminum door. And behold what a wonder, the colors outside had changed. The sea was blue-green-turquoise-glimmering-bright, and the sand had a yellowish-blue desert hue, like the colors you find in pictures and not in real life. In the distance, I saw animals from ancient times. They were running. There was one kind of animal with white fur. Its head was small compared to its size and it had a horn on its head. There was also a heavy, crude beast with legs that were thin compared to its body and it ran fast in circles. Suddenly the animal looked up and saw The Jew. It took a huge leap and landed on the veranda and approached him and licked the hand that was stretched out to it. He spoke to the creature affectionately, asked how it was doing, and said he was pleased that it had jumped up to visit. After that, another animal jumped in. It was small, with shaggy brown fur and a sort of mane covering its head. The Jew greeted it and said how good it was to see it, calling it Yekutiel. There were other ancient animals, the likes of which I had never seen. When I woke up I thought of Haim Be'er's wonderful book, *Back from the Heavenly Lack*, in which he wrote about our Jew, who was incarnated in his imagination in the form of a white yak. I thought of the ancient animals, whose form is both that of a yak and of a llama. I knew that there is a confusion of times here, and that these animals are indeed related to the essence of The Jew, and I understood that at the time we met, The Jew was engaged in elevating the souls of the scholars who were incarnated in strange animals.

DAYS FLY BY

Four Jewish Brides.

The four of them are dressed in white. Four beautiful, young, happy brides. Four smiling, laughing brides. A soft light illuminates them.

Two of them stand, the third is seated, and the fourth leans over her. They are preoccupied with themselves and unaware of what is happening around them. Their white clothes are no more than shrouds. White shrouds, some of them have crumbled. The four form a circle and start dancing, and their movements resemble floating.

Sheindel enters the circle, turns to me, and says, "I will tell you what happened to the world and to me after the death of My Jew."

And so Sheindel told me:

When My Jew died, we didn't even have a woolen prayer shawl to wrap his body in, because every time he had one in his possession, he would give it away to the poor, and when he prayed, he would wrap his body in a simple sheet with four tassels. And when he died, Yehoshua Asher dressed him in his own prayer shawl and hoped that his father would remember it favorably.

Many mourned his death. They said that the Holy Ark had been buried in Peshischa. They said he was like a prophet who saw through the illuminating mirror, a descendant of the angels, that he spoke sweet words of wisdom and was lovely and beloved. It was also said that he was as pure as the first man prior to the original sin. Simcha Bunim said he was like the golden sprig of wheat among the Righteous, just as Rabbi Akiva had been among the Tanaim, a wondrous, singular, and special sprig of wheat with seeds of gold.

The Seer was also saddened by the news of his death and said that The Jew had a great soul that had visited the world three times: in the soul of our forefather Jacob, in that of Mordechai the Jew, and also Rabeinu Tam, Jacob ben Meir, who also married the sister of his first wife.

I checked out what had been recorded in history about the battle at Leipzig, in preparation for which The Seer had sent The Jew to influence The Almighty. I learned that in that battle, Napoleon suffered his greatest defeat. About 500,000 soldiers fought one another; some 100,000 of them were killed or wounded. The battle symbolized France's defeat and ended Napoleon's first empire. But the Messiah did not come.

About six months after my husband's death, Napoleon was forced to give up his throne and was banished to Elba Island. Before Passover that same year, the righteous men, led by The Seer, decided to act to speed up the end. It was springtime, and the righteous men talked to one another and were reminded that just as Israel was saved in the spring when they went out of Egypt, so in the spring they would be rescued again. And what do the Hassids say? They tell us that The Seer enlisted the Holy Jew and The Preacher of Kozhnitz. On the eve of the holiday, the night of the

Seder, all the righteous men were supposed to be engaged in pursuing special spiritual intentions. But when The Jew sat with his family members and his followers to observe the Seder, I, Sheindel suddenly insisted on sitting next to him because I claimed that a wife's place is alongside her husband. I demanded that his mother, Matil, be respectful and move. Matil was offended and asked to remain in her seat, and The Jew tried to persuade me on the grounds of the commandment of honoring parents, but nothing helped because I, Sheindel, insisted. Oh – then Matil vacated the seat, but I continued to insist and demanded that Matil get up and leave the table because she had not immediately obliged me when I asked – and if my mother-in-law didn't get up from the Seder table, I threatened, I would not give out cushions for all the guests to recline on, because they had not listened to my request, and even argued with me. They said that I collected the reclining cushions and the pillows and would not agree to share them with the guests, and they were obliged to lean on their coats. Of course, in such a situation, The Jew could not pray nor direct his intentions to hasten the end. The unavoidable result was that the Messiah did not come that evening, all because of the suffering and hurt that I, Sheindel, had caused, since on that holy night, I committed the sin of pride – the worst of all the sins – because the source of pride is rooted in impurity.

"Do you understand? Because of me, the Messiah did not come. And it makes no difference that it happened on Passover, 1814, six months after my husband passed away!" Even after his death, they continued to speak evilly of me.

The effort to intervene in the supernal worlds greatly weakened the righteous men. The Preacher of Kozhnitz did not get out of bed for many days. He called himself "a bag of bones," stopped eating, and bitterly mourned the death of The Jew, and on the eve of the Festival of Tabernacles, or Sukkot, in 1814, about a year after his friend's passing, the Preacher of Kozhnitz also passed away.

There are those who say that Simchat Torah is a special day because it is the most suitable time for the coming of the Messiah. And indeed, on Simchat Torah, the year when The Preacher passed away The Seer was working to bring the Messiah and was so focused on doing so that something wonderous happened. He was sitting in his room on the top floor, a room with a window facing the market and the street. It was a very small window that no man could pass through.

The Seer wanted to focus all his attention on bringing the Messiah and asked his wife, Beilah, to watch over him. Suddenly she thought she heard a child shouting and crying for her help, so she hurried to open the door. She saw nothing outside except her husband's followers dancing in the street with great fervor. Beilah returned to The Seer's room and found it empty. The Hassids dancing in the street heard a dull sigh in the darkness of the night and saw a man lying in the street.

"Who are you?" they asked.

"I am Jacob Isaac, the son of Matil," the man replied.

And he told them that a great force suddenly came and threw him to the ground – through the window! They said that the fall occurred at the climax of the fierce battle between The Seer and Satan, who wanted to delay the coming of the Messiah. They picked him up and carried him to his room. And the window in the room was closed. The glasses that stood on the windowsill before these events remained in place.

And, as a result of his fall, The Seer was bedridden for a whole year until he died on the 9th Day of Av[25] of that same year. Before he died, he was angry that they had not told him that The Preacher had passed away because he had depended on his strength and support in that great battle and did not know that he would not be at his side to help him.

"If I had known that The Preacher was dead," he said, "I would not have entered those dangerous paths in the heavens above, and I would not have passed through the caves in the sky where the clouds, winds, lightning, thunder, and stars hide. And, even worse – the winding roads where the twisted forces of evil lie."

Only when he was struggling with the sinister powers that were hindering his advance did the souls of The Preacher and Matil, his mother, suddenly appear beside him in the supernal worlds, and did he understand that The Preacher was no longer among the living.

The Preacher spread his prayer shawl and secured The Seer from the right side, and his mother secured him from the left. In this way, they lessened the force of his fall. And he also said that had the Holy Jew – that's what he called him, Holy – still been alive, he would have prevented his fall altogether, and if all three of them had been together, there is no doubt that they would have brought Redemption to the world forever.

---

25. The day of the destruction of the first temple in 586 BCE and the second temple in 70 CE. According to the Sages, the Messiah will be born on the 9th day of the Hebrew month of Av.

In the space of a year, the three righteous men died. Some say that all this happened to them because they were burned by the holy flame of their actions to hasten the Redemption of the world.

After the death of my husband, The Jew, I began wandering among the small towns of Galicia, telling of his wonders. I traveled with my little son Nechemia in a kind of horse-drawn cart called a *badil*, because that was how the Hassids traveled in those days. Everywhere I stopped, I spoke about The Jew's marvels, and I received notes with petitionary prayers and requests (*kvitlach*) for healing, for becoming pregnant, and the like. I promised to pray to my husband and inform him of their requests, and assured them of relief through the powers of my husband, of blessed memory, may he rest in peace. This was because after their death – as I shamelessly promoted and explained – righteous men atone for Israel. And how do they atone? The righteous sit in the heavens above and look to see how their congregations of followers treat their family members. If their Hassids assure the family of the righteous man of a living – the righteous man will atone for their sins. And if they don't, he will say to himself,

"Why should I take their sins upon myself?"

I told stories of wonder and awe; through me, my husband's greatness became well-known, far and wide.

A woman wanders the roads by day and spends the nights with her six-year-old son in temporary lodgings.

Steamed-up window panes. You have to wipe them immediately to be able to see clearly whether there are dangers lurking on the way, if Cossacks are rushing about on horses, or if bandits are coming in the dark of night. Now it is especially important to keep a close eye on your little orphan son sleeping in a strange bed.

And this is what it's like: You give free rein to your fears, and instead of lying down and falling asleep, you stand and look at the gaping blackness in the window. You know that no good will come of it because what comes to a woman standing at a window and waiting? Only bad news comes to her, as happened to the mother of Sisera, whom Yael killed, and to Michal, Saul's daughter, who loved David and watched at the window, waiting for him to come. But he took other women instead of her.

So immediately, to avoid the decree of fate, you hurry and slip into the cold bed, trying to warm the toddler next to you with your embrace. On those nights, I would hug my son and think: When a person dies, what happens to his love after his death? Here, after Jacob Isaac, My Jew, died, I thought that at least at the end of his life there was love between us, but I realized that I no longer have a longing and desire for the love of another man, a living man, because I felt that Jacob Isaac's love remained with me, inside me, around me. I also felt great anger, anger that this love was not enough for me to be able to keep him here, to stop him from leaving.

When he came to me in my dreams, I didn't let him speak or even open his mouth. I just got angry and shouted, "Why? Why did you leave me?" And many nights I would wake up in tears and sometimes even scream, and I knew that I had once again missed the opportunity to hear what he had to say to me. He would come in the dreams of others and tell them things and give them advice and guide them about what they should do, even if they were complete strangers. Once, for example, when Yerachmiel and Yehoshua Asher fled from the soldiers who wanted to recruit them and hid outside in the bitter cold, The Jew came in a dream to a wealthy man who lived in the town and forced him to take care of the two boys. The man hid them in his house and took care of all their needs until the soldiers left.

But even when I don't dream of him, I know that the love I knew remains in me, a love that I did not believe in for many years, which was why I often got angry and came with complaints, but in the last days of Jacob Isaac's life, I witnessed its truth. And when I spoke to him during his life, I didn't always mean the things I said. Things that are said in anger are not always meant. Sometimes the anger rises and rises from within, at that point between the throat and the chest. And despite the quarrels that I started that allowed me to vent what was in my heart, it happened more than once that I suffered from such intense pain in my throat that the angry and painful things remained sealed inside me. And now, when it's cold outside, and gray and foggy, I feel how the thick air settles in my throat and the pain still hasn't come yet, but I know it will.

In the morning, I find the strength in myself that I don't have due to all the people who have already gathered to hear the amazing stories about The Jew. Some of these stories are also told about his sons; this also gives rise to the feeling that the stories are not always credible. But understand: Over the years, I started telling wonderful stories not only about My Jew, but also about his sons because it was important to me to take care of their future.

I was especially concerned about Nechemia, my youngest, who was only six when his father died, and that is why

I translated many of the stories about him – he also didn't leave a penny in his house overnight, didn't eat too much, and spoiled his food with salt and pepper. And I went further and also attributed to him some of the features of The Seer, who could look at people's foreheads and see all their incarnations. In his youth, he prayed to the Almighty in his goodness to free him of this difficult talent, and his prayer was answered. So I put him on equal footing with The Seer – who didn't want his eyesight. And I added and said that before his death, The Jew, predestined the youngest of his sons, Nechemia, to greatness. In addition, I did all that I could for my sons to assure them of their position and their resemblance to The Jew in his life as closely as possible.

Over the years, the stories also influenced the boys, who did not follow their father's way and adopted the way of miracles. Wearing his prayer shawl and phylacteries, Nechemia would cook fish in honor of Shabbat on a tiny ethanol flame and read all the notes containing requests that he had accumulated over the week while cooking the fish. And when healing the sick, he would whisper the phrase "Single spear swallowed, swallowed sharp spear," and said that he learned this whispered phrase from his father, The Holy Jew; The Jew himself learned the whispered phrase from the Angel Raphael, who is responsible for healing. He used the laws of *kashrut*, which determine whether an animal is kosher or not for consumption if it is unhealthy, to guide him in trying to cure patients with lung diseases. In complicated cases, he would open the Pentateuch and consult the Torah, which according to him was also a legacy from his father. He made great improvements in favor of the people of Israel with the help of The Jew's pipe that was bequeathed to him.

Although I was concerned about Nechemiah's fate, I loved Yehoshua Asher the most. When the children grew up, and Nechemiah left Peshischa and joined the Court of Rabbi Israel of Ruzhin, I got the idea of leaving Peshischa and moving in with my son Yehoshua Asher at his home in Zelichow. Yehoshua was married to Latzya, a descendent of the Baal Shem Tov, and as The Jew drew up the terms of the marriage agreement, it was decided that the wedding would be consecrated in the town of Lemberg, the home of the bride. Her father, Rabbi Hertzil was a very wealthy man, and they planned for all the important rabbis of the generation to attend – except The Jew knew this was likely to anger The Seer. When the enemies of The Jew heard what a great honor awaited him in Lemberg, they persuaded The Seer to give his blessing on condition that The Preacher of Kozhnitz would perform the marriage blessings in Lublin. And so instead of a sumptuous wedding, the ceremony was arranged without delay and was modest; even the father of the bride was not present.

But Latzya got sick, so to help my son take care of my daughter-in-law, I took up residence in Zelichow; even after her death I remained in the town and enjoyed the children born to him. My heart was attached to those children, and I wanted them to be as great as their father and grandfather; therefore I was told that in the early years, Yehoshua Asher and Latzya did not have children until The Jew blessed them with the four children that were intended to be born to him in this world, but were not because he reached such heights of holiness that he lost the urge for sexual relations. The four children born to Yehoshua Asher, I explained, are the four children that were not born to The Jew; indeed all four of them considered themselves to be the sons of their grandfather, The Jew, and they used to say *kaddish*[26] for him on the anniversary of his death. Three of them were the sons of Latzya, and the fourth was born to Yehoshua Asher, who after her death, married the granddaughter of The Seer of Lublin. And under the wedding canopy, so he said, stood his father, The Holy Jew, and The Seer of Lublin, and they both rejoiced at the union. And the son born of this marriage they called Meir Shalom, after the son of Beilah and The Seer of Lublin.

Don't be surprised by the presence of The Jew and The Seer of Lublin at the wedding. It was the custom of The Jew before and after his death, to attend the weddings of his sons and sons of his sons, as well as to concern and trouble himself that the matches would be good for his grandchildren; just as he participated in the celebrations after his death, so would he also sit and study with Simcha Bunim after his death. And so on one of the nights when he sat and studied, The Jew said to Simcha,

"I want your son Abraham as the bridegroom of my granddaughter Breindel." The Jew loved Abraham Moshe with all his heart because he discerned that his soul came down to him from a lofty source, and even Simcha Bunim attested to the fact that he stole his son's soul from the treasury stored under the throne of honor.

---

26. A prayer chanted by the mourners after the death of a parent, spouse, sibling, or child.

We raised little Breindel in our home because in those days it was accepted that grandchildren would live with their grandmother and grandfather if they were orphaned by the death of one of their parents. And from the day she was born, that little girl brought happiness to our hearts. She was so joyful, and her face was so delightful, and closely resembled Feigaleh, my deceased sister, except that her black hair was curly. And now My Jew is asking to make a match between the little one and the son of his disciple, who led the Hassids of Peshischa after him, Rabbi Simcha the pharmacist!

Simcha was overjoyed at the proposed marriage and immediately shook hands on it with The Jew. In the middle of the night, he went home and told his wife, Rivka, that he had arranged a marriage for their son. Right away, she began to yell at him. I have already mentioned that he would consult her about everything, so wasn't it strange that he was ignoring her opinion on this important matter? Avraham Moshe was her first-born son and the apple of her eye. More than once, she told me how on one of the coldest days in winter, when snow covered the paths, the sun suddenly peeked out of the thickets and she wanted the boy to see the splattered rays. He was an infant of about a year old, so she lifted him up toward the sky and glanced at his eyes, but he, instead of looking at the shimmering rays, stared into her eyes and smiled so brightly at her that her heart melted. Ever since, she loves the winter despite the fearful cold.

Rivka burst out screaming at Simcha, her husband, at how he had done this and thoughtlessly made a match for her son. Simcha answered her,

"Give me a moment to explain." She wept and said, "Some foolish Hassid probably came along and tempted you to marry our Avremeleh to his daughter."

Simcha told her, "This is not the case. I made the match with my teacher and Rabbi, The Jew. His granddaughter Breindel will marry our Avraham Moshe!"

Rivka's joy at the match was boundless. And I was also happy at the happy news of the marriage because I always loved Rivka, the wife of Rabbi Simcha, who helped me with her serene spirit and limitless patience in the stormy, early days of my marriage. And here my granddaughter Breindel was to marry her son! At the wedding festivities, all the guests stood awaiting the arrival of The Jew, my Jacob Isaac, for a long time, and did not begin the ceremony under the canopy until late. The waiting guests already had an appetite to taste the fine delicacies that had been prepared, and the young people were impatient for the melodies to start, all waiting and waiting until Rabbi Simcha felt the presence of The Jew, and raised his loud, clear voice:

"Welcome and blessed be my teacher and rabbi, the Holy Jew. Congratulations to you." And he began to intone the marriage blessings.

Because that is what My Jew promised – to bless the marriage of every couple of his descendants for seven generations.

"Married life is not easy. And who knows that better than us, my Sheindel?"

That is what he said when he told me of his decision, "and it wouldn't do any harm if I would also stand up and bless the couple with a good life, love, patience, and fertility."

When I was in Zelichow, I became especially close to

my granddaughter Raizel. I told you once that we look for ourselves in our children, and that also applies to our grandchildren. So I found myself in Raizel's steadfastness; in her wisdom and generosity, I found "My Jew." Years later, when she grew up, Raizel often gave to charity without her husband knowing about it.

When she was asked why she gives so much, since the Sages said not to give more than a fifth of your wealth to charity, she quoted the words of The Jew and replied, "True, but that is about someone who wants to fulfill the instructions of charity. But I am asking to atone for my sins, and he who atones for his sins, will give everything he has for his soul."

When they told her that her husband was angry with her because she squanders more money than she can afford, she replied that she had heard from her father who quoted the Holy Jew, that it was written in *Shulchan Aruch* (the compulsory rules of behavior) that a husband must heal his wife, "and when a poor man comes to my door, my heart breaks, and I oblige my husband to repair my broken heart – whatever the cost."

It seems that the days flew past me in a kind of stream that does not froth or bubble, but is similar to the flow of water that seeps through rock without leaving traces but by carving paths in it like rails, like the long furrows that go deeper and deeper on the sides of my jaw and neck, and tiny wrinkles in the thin and crumpled skin beside my eyes. And my eyes grew darker and my vision duller, so I asked my son Yehoshua Asher to buy me eyeglasses on his next trip to Lemberg.

As someone who has saved pennies all her life, and

calculated each day how to make them stretch to buy food for her children, I feel like a real sinner – that I can't make do with a loop, a kind of magnifying glass in the shape of a tube, a lens held to your eye, like Yerachmiel used when he fixed watches. No, I wasn't satisfied with a loop but indulged myself with a pair of glasses sold in the big city that have two arms tied with a velvet ribbon behind the head, and they make it possible to read without one's nose getting painfully pinched by the metal frame of the pince-nez.

And in the past year I had a spirit of childhood in me. I experienced almost everything as if for the first time. The heat of summer spread lethargy throughout my limbs, and I felt the silence of the afternoon and the rays of the blinding sun. I felt the urge to close my eyes and sense the quiet and warmth that had condensed in my body. I wanted to roll in the grass but didn't dare to, and so greatly regretted not having the courage to do so, but they had already cut the long stalks, and the scent of newly mowed grass was so powerful that I could taste it in my mouth. I wanted to experiment with things I had never experienced, and I promised myself never to allow the opinions of others determine what I would or would not do. I planned to continue to follow the custom of The Jew, who was never troubled by the opinion others held of him, and said that those who accept themselves are likely to be accepted by the whole world:

"Anyone who can laugh at oneself can laugh with all of mankind."

So when the snow came, I wore a hat, wound a warm scarf around my neck, put galoshes on my feet, and strode through the deep snow to the place where the young people skated on the ice; I even beckoned to one of them, a tall, slim, blue-eyed fellow, hinting to him that I wanted him to give me a ride on his sled. This was an unusual request, coming from an aging Jewish lady, because it isn't appropriate for Jewish women, maidens, or girls, to slide on a sled like reckless, mischievous kids. But my look of determination silenced objections that were not even raised, and I sat on the sled and gave myself up to the speed and the freezing wind on my cheeks. Suddenly the sled stopped, swerving to the right, and I heard a man's voice, interrogating the youngster, who remained silent and just glanced at me as though he knew and understood, and I looked at the puzzled man and gave him a meaningful glance, implying things that were beyond his understanding, and which I could not explain to him. The man lowered his gaze and I motioned to the lad with my hand to continue taking me for a ride on the sled. I wanted to experience everything and did not know what the day still had in store for me.

A MOTHER'S MERCY

Four Jewish Brides.

The four of them are dressed in white. Four beautiful, young, happy brides. Four smiling, laughing brides. A soft light illuminates them.

Two of them stand, the third is seated, and the fourth leans over her. They are preoccupied with themselves and unaware of what is happening around them. Their white clothes are no more than shrouds. White shrouds, some of them have crumbled. The four form a circle and start dancing, and their movements resemble floating.

Sheindel enters the circle. And bids farewell:

I have told you the stories of four women. Four women who married the righteous men of the generation, whose names were identical: Jacob Isaac, The Seer of Lublin, and Jacob Isaac, The Jew of Peshischa. In my story, I did not attempt to describe them as if they were saints. I described them as they were, with their good and bad attributes, and all I wanted was to rescue them from the background – the background in which their part was to emphasize by contrast the righteousness of their husbands and give them their own point of view, and voice. In the stories that the Hassids told about them, the emphasis was on the judgment, and not the mercy. While I came to tell their stories,

I did not want to lie or beautify, but to emphasize mercy over judgment – mercy in the language of motherhood, of the womb, whose principles are superior to those of fiery rigid principles and fanatical ideology.

And mostly, I wanted to express a female point of view, because every person, male or female, is one of a kind, and therefore wives of righteous men fight to be themselves, and not just a pristine mirror that reflects the image of their men.

That is what Sheindel tells me and leaves the circle.

And in the month of Shvat 1851 – some thirty-seven years after Her Jew – Sheindel, aged about seventy, passed away.

Made in United States
North Haven, CT
06 May 2024

52178563R00107